Katie cleared her throat and forced herself to ask anyway. "I have a proposition for you."

One jet-black eyebrow arched. "How intriguing."

Alessandro's tone couldn't sound less intrigued or any more dismissive.

Irritation stiffened her; she was too desperate to cope with casual dismissal. "I work at White Oaks," she carried on. "I've developed sauces made from our produce. They sell very well."

She paused because so far, he was so bored looking. Her desperation swiftly blew up to all-out pain.

"Cut to the chase, Katie," he drawled. "What do you want from me?"

She was so thrown by the reality of Alessandro in the flesh, so intimidated by that look in his eyes that she forgot the little speech she'd carefully prepared to try to convince him. It just tumbled out with no further preamble.

"I want you to marry me."

Conveniently Wed!

Conveniently wedded, passionately bedded!

Whether there's a debt to be paid, a will to be obeyed or a business to be saved...she's got no choice but to say, "I do!"

But these billionaire bridegrooms have got another think coming if they imagine marriage will be that easy...

Soon their convenient brides become the objects of inconvenient desire!

Find out what happens after the vows in:

Chosen as the Sheikh's Royal Bride
by Jennie Lucas

Penniless Virgin to Sicilian's Bride
by Melanie Milburne

Untamed Billionaire's Innocent Bride
by Caitlin Crews

Bought Bride for the Argentinian
by Sharon Kendrick

Contracted as His Cinderella Bride
by Heidi Rice

Shock Marriage for the Powerful Spaniard
by Cathy Williams

Look for more Conveniently Wed! stories coming soon!

Natalie Anderson

THE INNOCENT'S EMERGENCY WEDDING

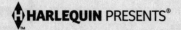

Recycling programs
for this product may
not exist in your area.

ISBN-13: 978-1-335-47871-9

The Innocent's Emergency Wedding

First North American publication 2019

Copyright © 2019 by Natalie Anderson

Printed in U.S.A.

www.Harlequin.com

USA TODAY bestselling author **Natalie Anderson** writes emotional contemporary romance full of sparkling banter, sizzling heat and uplifting endings—perfect for readers who love to escape with empowered heroines and arrogant alphas who are too sexy for their own good.

When she's not writing, you'll find Natalie wrangling her four children, three cats, two goldfish and one dog...and snuggled in a heap on the sofa with her husband at the end of the day.

Follow her at www.natalie-anderson.com.

Books by Natalie Anderson

Harlequin Presents

Claiming His Convenient Fiancée
The Forgotten Gallo Bride
The King's Captive Virgin
Awakening His Innocent Cinderella
Pregnant by the Commanding Greek

One Night With Consequences

Princess's Pregnancy Secret

The Throne of San Felipe

The Secret That Shocked De Santis
The Mistress That Tamed De Santis

Visit the Author Profile page at Harlequin.com for more titles.

For the gorgeous Alfie; you're such a loyal four-legged friend, the exclamation point completing our family and the best foot warmer a writer could have.

CHAPTER ONE

'You can't make me marry him. You can't make me marry anyone...'

Katie Collins perched nervously on the plush chair in the vast reception room of Zed Enterprises, gripping her bag and reminding herself to breathe often enough to remain conscious. If she'd had more pride—or any other option—she'd have walked out over an hour ago, but the threats relentlessly circling in her head had forced her to remain. He was the one person who had the power to help.

'If you won't marry him you can leave right now, and you know that would kill her—'

Katie blinked the horror away and focused on her surroundings. Alessandro Zetticci's offices showcased a sleek, minimalist style—steel and chrome screamed masculine sophistication and the wealth he'd accumulated in an astoundingly short time. It didn't surprise her. He'd always had the knack of knowing what people wanted.

It had been a decade since she'd seen him and, while certain aspects of that particular visit were branded in her brain, she was acutely aware that he mightn't even remember who she was. She'd have to remind him before begging for his benevolence.

'You'll be homeless. So will the woman who's spent years caring for you, you ungrateful little b—'

Katie again blocked the echo of the viciousness her foster father had spat at her. Seeking distraction, she glanced at the receptionist. Dressed in a sleek navy skirt and smooth white blouse, the tall blonde looked like a chic French movie star, ageing with impossible grace. Katie was also wearing a navy skirt with a white blouse, but where the receptionist's was silk, Katie's was synthetic, and right now it was sticking to her. Outclassed, out of place…she was never quite good enough—

Katie stiffened, snapping out of the self-pity. She didn't need fancy clothes, given she worked in the orchards and the kitchen most of the time.

'You can't refuse after all I've done for you—'

A trickle of sweat slithered down her back, even though the building was beautifully climate-controlled. Her body was literally leaking her nerves. She uncurled her grip on her bag for the twentieth time. Only to immediately clutch the strap again as if it were her lifeline.

She'd not made an appointment, and it was sheer luck that Alessandro was in the office at all today. Too late she realised she had no idea what she'd have done if he hadn't been. She still had no idea what she was going to do if he said no.

'Don't you want to be a real member of the family?'

That attempt at manipulation had stabbed deep. So after all this time Katie was still an outsider? She'd always felt Brian hadn't wanted her, but for him to state it so explicitly, for him to try to force her into doing something insane… She was still an outsider. Still just someone who *owed*...

'Do you want to watch her devastation?'

And that was the problem. She did owe Susan, her foster mother. She more than owed her—she loved her, and she had to protect her.

'Ms Collins?' The elegant receptionist finally interrupted her anxious reverie. 'Alessandro is ready to see you now.'

Katie's heart skidded. She was seized with the urge to bolt in the other direction. Instead she followed the older woman, drawing in a deep breath as she went.

It was a good thing she did, because the second she walked into his office her lungs, like the rest of her, were rendered immobile. She'd looked at recent pictures on the train ride here, so she'd thought she'd be immune. She'd been wrong. Alessandro Zetticci in the flesh was overwhelming.

Katie couldn't smile as the receptionist left—couldn't even see what the room was like, because she couldn't peel her gaze from where he stood behind his desk. Flashes of rogue memory burned. Alessandro in the orchard. His smile. His low laugh. His broad shoulders…

She blinked, desperately focusing on him here and now and *clothed*.

His jet-black hair was straight and long enough to flop in his eyes. His sculpted cheekbones were emphasised by the razor-sharp edge of a perfectly symmetrical, masculine jaw. Lightly stubbled rather than clean-shaven, he looked as if it wasn't long since he'd left his bed. Long black lashes and dark eyebrows framed his arresting eyes. Powder blue, they were brightly backlit by fierce burning intensity.

If she hadn't known better she'd have thought he wore coloured contact lenses, but Katie had seen him sullen and silent over the breakfast table and at Christmas dinners long gone by, and even then, when he'd been moody and resentful, his eyes had glowed with that brilliance.

His mouth had a natural sinful curve, a permanent wicked half-smile—as if he were thinking something slightly inappropriate. It was a mouth made to kiss. Katie remembered that.

The top button of his white shirt was undone, exposing a deeply tanned neck. That tan was an all-over one. Katie remembered that too.

The man was appallingly handsome. The kind of gorgeous rarely seen in the streets, that made ordinary people turn for a second, third, fourth look.

But it wasn't only his smouldering looks that drew people's attention. It was the energy that crackled from him. He had vitality—a kind of fire that drew everyone around him in. It was what had made his empire so massive, so quickly. Because of that smile and that aura of amusement, everyone wanted to lean closer, seduced by the self-assurance that glowed in his eyes.

More than self-assurance he had arrogance—a pure don't-give-a-damn attitude that made him impossibly popular and his investments an unparalleled triumph. He looked ready for something far more enjoyable and intimate than business. He looked like a man with a wicked ability to have a good time. And he followed through on that appearance. He was irresistible—catnip to pretty much every woman in the world. And he was happy to be played with. But never caught.

Katie *definitely* remembered that.

Yet Alessandro Zetticci had faced hardship too. Katie was counting on that fact to make him human. Make him understand. Make him want to *help*.

Now she blinked again, breaking the mortifying immobility his appearance had engendered and stepped deeper into his domain. He didn't greet her—didn't say anything. His swift glance seemed to take her in and dismiss her all in one second.

'I'm Katie Collins,' she began, her embarrassment blooming in the face of his uncharacteristic frigidity. 'I live at White Oaks Hall with Brian Fielding—'

He still didn't smile. 'I don't need you to remind me who you are, Katie.'

'I wasn't sure you'd remember—'

'How could I possibly forget?' Displeasure and disapproval flashed in his eyes.

Faltering at his unfriendly demeanour, Katie licked her dry lips. She'd done nothing to him. Certainly she'd *meant* nothing to him.

Alessandro Zetticci had stalked into Katie's life when he was a sullen fifteen and she a very shy ten. His father, famed Italian chef Aldo Zetticci, had just married Brian's sister Naomi. Brian and Naomi were close, so Aldo and Alessandro had joined the extended Fielding family for holidays at White Oaks—much to Alessandro's obvious resentment.

Only a couple of years later Aldo had died. Alessandro and Naomi had then clashed on the future of his father's food empire. Brian had backed Naomi. Petulant and fiery, Alessandro had fought hard, flaring up at Brian's interference.

'If you go now, you'll never be welcome back here.'

Brian's banishment of Alessandro had terrified her at the time.

'Don't mention him again.'

Brian had whirled on her when she'd fearfully asked where Alessandro had gone. She'd been too young to understand everything, but had known that in no way had it all been Alessandro's fault. In any case, Alessandro's ideas for his father's company couldn't have been that bad, given he'd gone on to build his own business with such success.

He'd always been determined and strong. But from the look in his eyes now he was also unforgiving.

Katie cleared her throat and forced herself to speak anyway. 'I have a proposition for you.'

One jet-black eyebrow arched. 'How intriguing.'

His tone couldn't have sounded *less* intrigued or any more dismissive.

Irritation stiffened her. She was too desperate to cope with casual dismissal. 'I work at White Oaks,' she carried on. 'I've developed some sauces made from our produce. They sell very well.'

She paused, because so far he was bored-looking. Her desperation swiftly blew up to all-out pain.

'Cut to the chase, Katie,' he drawled. 'What do you want from me?'

She was so thrown by the reality of Alessandro in the flesh, so intimidated by that look in his eyes, that she forgot the little speech she'd carefully prepared to try to convince him. It just tumbled out with no further preamble.

'I want you to marry me.'

His eyes widened, the black heart of his pupils all

but swallowed the fiery brilliant blue. The rest of him didn't move. He didn't even seem to be breathing.

'Not for real of course,' she hastened to add awkwardly. 'In name only. And not for long.'

'You want me to marry you?' he repeated slowly. 'That was *not* what I expected you to say.'

Katie tensed, unable to read his expression, but then he threw back his unfairly handsome head and laughed. It seemed he'd not heard anything as entertaining in eons. And it was utterly insulting.

Scalding emotion curdled the raw acid in Katie's stomach. All her life she'd strived to meet everyone else's requests and demands as she'd desperately tried to fit in and stay safe. But in this instance she was sick of staying silent and being good. Because almost no one ever asked what *she* wanted.

Fury filled her, fuelled by total humiliation. 'I'm so glad I could give you a joke for the day,' she spat sarcastically. 'Forget I ever said anything.'

'I'm unlikely to ever forget that.'

He strolled around his desk with deceptively casual strides, swiftly moving to where she stood, only three feet into his office.

'What are you doing?' Her voice veered up in an embarrassing squawk as he stepped deep into her personal space.

He didn't reply. Instead he surveyed her dispassionately, rather as if she was a curiosity in a natural history museum. Then he leaned closer still.

'Are you *sniffing* me?' Outraged, she flinched away from him.

'Yes. Have you been drinking?' He reached out and grasped her chin.

Katie stilled, attempting to fix him with a furious gaze.

Unconcerned, he turned her face to one side then the other, intently studying her features. 'On drugs?'

'What? *No.*' She jerked free of his hold. 'Look, I'm perfectly sane.' The truth slipped out, and so did all the hurt and hopelessness. 'I'm just in trouble, and you're the only person I could think of who might be able to help me. Obviously you can't, so I'll leave now.'

She turned sharply as emotions whacked her with a one-two punch. She'd never been as embarrassed or as violently angry. She suddenly spun back, slamming her fury into his face.

'I don't know why I thought *you'd* understand the desire to protect the person you love most—to prevent her losing the thing she loves more than anything,' she yelled at him. 'I don't know why I thought *you'd* ever understand that!'

He stared at her for a long second, his mouth compressed. Sudden emotion flared in his eyes and he stepped forward. 'Katie—'

She shoved past him, rage giving her strength, but just as she reached the door he slammed his hand high above hers to hold it shut, stopping her from storming out. She tugged, but couldn't beat his weight or strength and the door remained sealed. She tugged harder.

'Katie, stop,' he said eventually.

Belatedly she stilled, realising too late what an exhibition she was making of herself. She breathed hard, trying to block the sensations caused by his invasion of her personal space. He was right behind her, leaning so close she could feel his heat. Something insidious shifted inside her. Something deep…something tempting. Something she intuitively knew she needed to ignore.

She closed her eyes in embarrassment.

'You can't just storm in, demand something so outrageous and then flounce off without an explanation. You need to speak,' he added firmly. 'Sit down and start from the beginning.'

She remained locked in place for another mortified moment. He was right. And she'd been so wrong. She should never have come—what had she been thinking?

But he wasn't going to let her leave without a proper explanation. And didn't she owe him that at least? Hell, she was every bit the useless idiot Brian had called her...

Slowly she released the door handle and pivoted awkwardly on the spot. Because Alessandro didn't stand back to give her room to move. He still had his palm pressed on the door, as if he didn't trust her not to try to escape again. He was still so close she almost felt giddy.

Breathe, Katie, breathe.

But she was looking into his eyes and all kinds of confusion clouded her mind. She'd been such a fool to think she could handle him.

He gazed at her, his clear blue eyes compelling and uncharacteristically serious. 'Take a seat and talk to me.'

He suddenly swung aside so she could walk back into the room.

She quickly bypassed him and sank into the nearest chair, her knees strangely wobbly. 'White Oaks is in debt,' she said in a low voice. 'Apparently we're about to lose it. Susan doesn't know.'

'But isn't it Susan's estate?' Alessandro folded his

arms and leaned back against the door, still blocking the exit.

'Yes.'

Her foster mother had lived there all her life—had inherited it upon her parents' death. And now, as she faced the disease that was slowly killing her, it was her sanctuary. Katie couldn't sit back and watch Susan lose it.

'But she left the business side of it to Brian when her health began to deteriorate. She focused on the gardens—you know she loves them. All these years…'

She shook her head. She'd had no idea that the estate finances were so dire—that Brian had mismanaged everything so badly and hidden it, to boot. His betrayal hurt.

'He only told me the depth of the trouble we're in yesterday.'

Katie couldn't let Susan lose all that was her love and her life. She'd thought the garden tours she'd organised and the sauce business she'd started would be enough to keep the books she'd seen balanced, but she'd been wrong.

'Brian says he's made a deal. If I marry Carl Westin, Carl will absorb our debt and Susan and Brian can stay at White Oaks.'

'If you marry Carl Westin?' Alessandro pushed away from the door and walked towards her, his gaze narrowing. 'Of Westin Processing?'

'You know him?'

Alessandro looked shocked. 'He's only a little younger than Brian—'

'And a lot older than me, yes.'

'Not to mention unreliable and—'

'Creepy,' she interrupted fiercely. 'I can't marry him.'

Alessandro rubbed his hand across his mouth, hiding the smile that felled a thousand women. 'This is twenty-first-century London, Katie. I don't think Brian can bully you into a marriage you don't want.'

Discomfort clawed at her innards. Alessandro didn't know the subtle ways in which her foster father had undermined her over the years. How did she explain something so complex? Explain that something so important had been shredded by stealth over time? By subtle comments and control?

'There's physical force, but then there's the more emotional kind…' Her throat tightened, shame silencing her. She hated her powerlessness, her lack of real *strength*.

The remnants of his smile faded as he watched her struggle to finish her sentence. 'Your supposed debt to Susan?'

It wasn't 'supposed'. Susan had cared for Katie. She was the first—the only—person to have done that.

Katie had gone to them when she was almost two, when Susan had finally got Brian to agree to fostering after they'd spent years trying for children of their own. But Brian had never agreed to adoption, and there'd always been the threat that Katie could be sent back into the care system.

In truth, Brian was as controlling of Susan as he was of Katie. It was only that Susan seemed mostly blind to it.

'She's vulnerable.' She glanced at Alessandro. 'She's in a wheelchair now. She can't be left alone for long.'

As Susan's neurological disease progressed, she lived in her own world, safe in the grounds of the estate. A world Katie cared for with her.

'It would kill her to have to leave White Oaks.' Katie had to keep it secure for Susan until the end. 'It's her life.'

She loved her gentle foster mother dearly. Susan had welcomed her, and they'd spent so much time together sheltered on the estate... Though over the last decade their roles had slowly reversed. Katie now read to Susan, kept her company and comfortable. She'd do almost anything for her.

But Katie couldn't talk to Susan about how bad things had become financially, or about Brian's insane plan—she was too fragile to be burdened with that. For a while now Katie had been shielding Susan from several problems Brian had wrought.

'So, if Carl gets you, White Oaks stays safe for Susan.' Alessandro summed it up bluntly. 'But why does Carl want you?'

She flinched, hit by a hot flash of embarrassment. Yeah, she was hardly catch of the day. 'You don't think he finds me attractive?' she mumbled, knowing her face was blushing beetroot.

He had the grace to shoot her a rueful look. 'If he actually *wanted* you he wouldn't woo you with an ultimatum like this.'

'Maybe he can't get anyone else to say yes to him? Maybe he thinks he'll get an obedient wife?' she said bitterly. 'This way he'll be able to control me. He's used to getting what he wants, however he has to do it.'

Alessandro stepped towards her, the whisker of a smile in his eyes. 'And you think I'm different?'

A hot fury built within her. 'I'm sure you're used to getting what you want. Fortunately you don't want me.'

He blinked and that smile fully resurfaced. 'How do you know I don't want you?'

She laughed bitterly. 'You never so much as looked at me.'

'If I recall, the last time we met you were little more than a child. It would have been unacceptable in every way if I'd looked at you then.' He angled his head. 'But I'm looking at you now.'

As if that was going to make any difference!

'Don't bother,' she snapped. 'You have hundreds of gorgeous women you really want. All of them. At once—' She broke off, realising she'd got herself into a quagmire of excruciating embarrassment.

'Hundreds at once?' he echoed with mild incredulity.

'Oh, whatever.' She shook off his amusement. 'You know you don't need to threaten a woman to get your way with her. You don't need to use blackmail—emotional or otherwise.'

'But that's what Brian does to you.' All amusement had dropped from his expression.

She drew in a deep breath and sighed. 'He's used to me doing what he says.'

Because she'd always worked to keep the peace, for Susan. But in asking this of her Brian had gone too far. It wasn't a business deal he'd arranged, it was marriage—intimate and personal. And Brian's brutal response to her refusal had horrified her. So she'd decided to figure out a deal of her own with the one man Brian despised. The only man she'd been able to think of.

'But you're not his daughter,' Alessandro said.

'Thank you for that reminder,' she said stiffly, swallowing back the burn of pain.

It was stupid how much it hurt. There'd always been those little comments from Brian—constantly reminding her that she wasn't family, that she had to be grateful and good, keep her on her best behaviour... The few times she'd tried to fight back, he'd squashed her.

'I'm no blood relative to *any* of them.'

And that was what gave Brian even more power over her.

'You don't think of me as family?' Alessandro asked.

She glanced up at him. 'You weren't there. How could you be?'

Alessandro had only appeared from boarding school during holidays and formal occasions. Her aloof 'step-cousin' couldn't have been less interested in forming a relationship with his new family.

'And thank you for *that* reminder,' he echoed with a soft jeer. An arrogant smile curved his lips for a fleeting second. 'I chose to leave—why can't you?'

'I'm not like you,' she said. 'I can't just walk out. I can't talk to Susan about it—she doesn't know about any of this.' Katie was protecting her on several levels. 'I'd buy out the debt myself, if I could, but I have hardly any money.'

His gaze narrowed. 'You said your sauces sell well?'

She bristled at his belittling tone. 'They do okay. They're even stocked in Sybarite, here in London.'

She'd been so delighted when the gourmet deli had put in a repeat order only a week ago, taking almost all her stock.

'Sybarite? Wonderful.' He said with light mockery. 'Then why aren't you paid accordingly?'

'I put all the profit back into the business... I don't need a lot personally.'

His eyebrows shot up.

'I live in,' she explained irritably. 'I have accommodation and food. I don't need fancy things.'

He skimmed a glance over her outfit and she shrank at the hint of disdain in his eyes.

But then she fought back. 'I knew things weren't good—that's why I started the garden tours as well. I owe it to them to work hard...to help Susan.'

She'd heard that phrase so many times and Brian was right, she *did* owe them. They'd plucked her from a life of poverty and neglect... Who knew what her life would have been like if it hadn't been for their generosity?

'You don't owe them the rest of your life,' Alessandro said bluntly.

'No, but I love Susan,' she said fiercely. 'And she *needs* me now.'

'There's no one else? Not her husband?' he said dryly.

Katie froze at the disparagement in his tone. 'All the times I've tried to stand up to Brian... In the end I've given in...'

'Because of Susan?'

'Yes.'

But Alessandro was right, wasn't he? She didn't have to sacrifice her whole life.

'I guess because of her...he has a hold over me,' she said lamely.

'And I don't?'

'Of course not.'

But she couldn't meet Alessandro's eyes. He had a hold over her in a way that she could never admit to herself, let alone to him.

'So you think that if you marry someone else then you won't have to marry Carl?'

'Yes.'

But when he put it as baldly as that it sounded crazy.

'Why me?' he asked.

'Because you're outrageous enough to actually do it,' she said bluntly.

No one would expect the infamous playboy to settle, and somehow she thought he might enjoy that unpredictability.

'And, according to the rich list, you have more money than you know what to do with.'

'Now, *that's* what I originally expected.' His twisting smile held little mirth. 'You want me to rescue White Oaks financially? Why not just ask me for the money? Why do we have to marry?'

'Because it's a language Brian understands. If I'm not married—without the protection of a *man*,' she spat sarcastically, 'I'll still be controllable. If I'm married, he'll back off. I don't want just to be out of reach. I want to be repulsive.'

'Repulsive?' Alessandro echoed awfully. 'And there's no better way to do that than by marrying *me*? Wow.' He leaned forward. 'You make it sound so eighteenth-century... Will you be sullied for ever if you're with me?'

'*Married* to you, yes.'

She'd never forgotten the look of anger on Brian's face when he'd seen an article featuring Alessandro in the newspapers.

'Brian will hate that I've come to you.'

He drew in a sharp breath.

Katie suddenly realised what she's said and sent him a contrite look. 'I'm sorry—'

'Don't apologise for being honest.' He watched her for a moment. 'You'll do anything to look after Susan?'

'Almost anything.' A welter of guilt swamped Katie.

His sympathetic glance was laced with sarcasm. 'You'd rather sell yourself to a wealthy tyrant of your own choosing?'

'That's right.'

'So, between Carl and me, I'm the lesser of two evils? The more attractive?'

A frisson of danger lent steel to his light query. She suddenly felt afraid of something, felt fear slicing through her too sensitive, too thin skin.

'You're temporary,' she said bravely. 'You like temporary. You never hold on to anything for long. Not women or companies. You take what you want and move on.'

'You really think you've done your research on me, don't you?' He looked down at her, grimly thoughtful. 'How can you go back there if you defy Brian so overtly?'

'I think he'll accept it when he realises his financial problems are resolved. And he'll see he can't reach me any more.' She'd finally be free of his hold over her.

'But what will Susan say about you marrying me for my money? Me, the spurned step-nephew, cast out all those years ago? Won't she be disappointed in you?'

A flush of heat singed her skin. 'I wouldn't tell her... I'd have to...'

'Fake it?' he jeered softly. 'Pretend you're in love with me?'

'It wouldn't be for long. Then White Oaks will be safe and Susan can stay there for as long as she has left.

Brian can't bully us into anything. He can't send either of us away if I own it. I'll have the power.'

Alessandro regarded her steadily. 'Sounds like a fine plan when you put it like that.' He hunched down in front of her and whispered. 'But what's in it for *me*?'

She stared into his gleaming eyes, wondering how to convince him—playing to his sympathetic side seemed unlikely to succeed. 'I thought you might enjoy it…' she muttered.

'What—being married to you?' That tantalising smile curved his lips, all arrogance.

She blushed furiously. 'Having revenge on *them*.'

He pressed his hand to his heart in mock distress. 'You really don't think much of me, do you?' he said slowly, but that edge was still in his eyes.

'You don't want to take something from them when they took something from you?'

That glint sharpened. 'What do you think they took?'

'Your father's company.' She swallowed, remembering that fight and the fury with which Alessandro had stormed out of White Oaks.

There was a moment of pure stillness. She couldn't tell what he was thinking behind those fiercely burning eyes. She only knew that he was thinking rapidly—but what he was thinking was clear only to him.

'Hasn't all your research told you I'm more successful than they are now?' he asked sharply, standing up and stepping back from her. 'I don't waste my time thinking about the past. I don't need their business. I don't need your sauces. And I certainly don't need your insane proposal.'

His rejection hit her in a low, dulling blow. Of course he didn't. Of course she couldn't convince him. She was a fool for having thought this could work, but it had been her only plan. She'd been desperate. She still was desperate.

But in the face of his displeasure she fell back into her automatic safety mode. 'Sorry,' she muttered tonelessly. She'd been conditioned for years to apologise when confronted with conflict. 'I'm so sorry.'

Angrily, he muttered something in Italian. Something that sounded viciously impolite. 'What did you *think* was going to happen here today?'

She had no clue. She'd not really thought at all. The mad idea had come to her in the middle of the night. He was the only man she knew with the resources, maybe the motivation, and truthfully he had been her only hope. So she'd sneaked out early in the morning and caught the first train to London.

'What does Carl say about it?' Alessandro almost snarled. 'Does he know the bride he's buying is so unwilling? Can't you bargain a better deal with him?'

'He came to see me last night.' Her skin crawled at the thought of Carl and what he'd said to her. 'I'd hoped he meant for us to be married in name only, but…'

'He wants you to have his babies?' Alessandro's whole demeanour seemed to sharpen.

It wasn't funny, it was foul, and it made her escape all the more imperative. 'He said he'll take what he wants.'

And apparently he did want her…*like that*.

Alessandro swiftly strode further away from her. 'But you don't want him?'

'Of course I don't!' The thought repulsed her.

Alessandro stood on the other side of his desk, leaning on it. There was a moment as he studied her. She saw him take a careful breath.

'What if you were to marry me?' His expression turned speculative. 'You wouldn't want to—?'

'No!' she interrupted vehemently.

'No?' He smiled at the interruption, and that crooked curve to his mouth was sinful. 'What if *I* wanted to?'

It was horrendous how attractive his smile was—and that lightness to his eyes…

'Really? Does your ego need to get any bigger?' She glared at him.

He'd already said no to her. She already knew he wasn't interested. He was just teasing her now—his amusement was audible.

'We both know you have millions of other options,' she said, completely flustered. 'I wouldn't get in your way.'

His eyebrows shot up. 'Wouldn't you?' he asked dryly, before a soft laugh escaped him. 'You as my wife would be willing to just stand by and watch me with other women?'

She flushed, her brain sending her that one image she'd successfully blocked for years—until today. Because she *had* watched him with another woman once.

She'd come across them accidentally. She'd been walking through the orchards, alone as always, when she'd spotted them lying in a grassy patch beneath a heavily flowering apricot tree. He had been shirtless and his jeans had been undone, slipping down his thighs. The muscles of his broad, bronzed back had moved powerfully as he'd bent over the pretty student who'd been arched beneath him.

Her sighing whispers had been too soft for Katie to decipher from that distance. But she'd heard the wickedness in the tone of his low, murmured reply and the breathless, rapid response of the woman he was bestowing carnal pleasure upon. He'd literally been devouring her.

Katie had frozen—not even hiding—fascinated and appalled at the sight of such complete intimacy— at his raw masculinity. She'd been an extremely sheltered young teen, still figuring things out and not really understanding what she was seeing.

To be honest, she still didn't understand it. She'd never met a man who'd made her want to act so wantonly despite the threat of exposure. To be that hedonistic, that caught up in a moment that she wouldn't care who was around to watch...

After only seconds she'd fled, with the sounds of that woman's delight echoing in her ears.

She'd told herself it wasn't her fault. If he was going to pleasure his girlfriend in the orchard—where anyone could have seen them—well, that was his problem. But she'd flushed almost purple that night, when he'd finally graced them with his presence at dinner that evening, almost half an hour late.

'Got held up,' he'd offered—not an apology, just a careless fact.

She'd seen him again in the village a few days later—with a different girl hungrily kissing him in an alleyway. His apparent infidelity to that first girl had shocked her. There'd been another girl only a couple of days later.

It had taken the young and naive Katie a while to realise he wasn't actually in a relationship with any of them. No commitment, no mess—only fun. Alessandro had been incredibly popular and he hadn't been afraid to make the most of it.

And it seemed every woman who'd crossed his path since was as eager to slide her legs apart and let him do whatever he liked between them... He hadn't slowed down any in the decade since that last summer he'd come to the estate.

Katie's quick Internet search on the train this morning had thrown up a billion pictures of him with a billion different women. All beautiful. All as enthusiastic as anything, judging by the look in their eyes. Alessandro Zetticci was an insatiable, arrogant playboy. Which actually made him perfect.

But he wasn't having her. She wasn't interested in any of that.

Only now he'd rounded his desk again. He gripped the armrests of her chair, bending so that his nose was only inches from her own. Dawning brilliance lit his eyes.

'Would you watch, Katie?' he asked.

Did he somehow know about that awful, embarrassing secret of her past?

'You're trying to intimidate me,' she squeaked. 'It's not going to work. I'm not afraid of you.'

He laughed. 'Perhaps you should be. But perhaps I'm not trying to intimidate you. Perhaps I'm testing you.'

'For what?'

He lifted a hand, lightly exploring her jawline with the lightest touch. 'To see if I can seduce you.'

His touch ought to have been easily escapable, but she couldn't seem to move.

Desperately she quelled the flare of heat deep and low in her belly and deliberately rolled her eyes. 'Sorry. I'm immune. That's why we'd be perfect together.'

'I agree,' he answered urbanely, but his eyes danced with devilish laughter. 'Perfect together. In bed.'

'I'm *not* going to sleep with you.'

'So determined…' His lips curled. 'Afraid you might catch something?'

It was a low, teasing drawl, but there was a sharp warning underlying his tone that made her wary. She'd been offensively rude in her outright rejection of any kind of intimacy with him. But as if it was even a consideration! He was the one being rude now.

You did just ask him to marry you.

And she had implied that he was a complete man whore.

'No.' She flushed uncomfortably, because he kept switching from serious to teasing. 'I'm just—'

'Scared you might like it?' he interpolated with a low chuckle.

Yes, this was the Alessandro Zetticci she'd read about—the irrepressible tease who worked hard but played harder.

'You really can't help yourself, can you?' She glared at him in exasperation. 'You think you can seduce every woman you meet!'

'Most don't need to be seduced.' He shrugged, then muttered with outrageous insouciance, 'Most are willing to let me do whatever I want before I even know their name.'

He was so close his words whispered over her lips… so close he seemed to see all her secrets. She closed her eyes—only to regret it instantly. Because now she was even more attuned to his nearness. His heat. His strength. His will. But she knew his words were designed to shock her, to repulse her. Because beneath the seductive slide of his whisper she still heard that steely anger.

She opened her eyes and glared at him. 'I'm not most women. And I'm not challenging you. This isn't about that and never will be.' She drew in a deep breath. 'If we marry I'll have no expectations, put no restrictions on you. And I'd expect the same for you.'

He straightened, and from his towering height shot her a censorious look as if he'd suddenly become the epitome of virtue.

'I may be many things, but a breaker of promises I am not. Even in a civil ceremony I'd promise fidelity, and I'd never break that promise. If you want me to marry you, you'd better agree to the same.' He was very curt and very clear.

She slammed her hands on the arms of the chair to stop herself slithering down to the floor. Was he going to say yes?

'You'd—?'

'Honour our vows for the duration of our marriage. Of course.'

'But—'

'Does it really come as that much of a shock?' He pinched the bridge of his nose.

'It's just that you—'

'I've never got married before? No. Never had the desire nor reason to.'

Her jaw hung open. 'Are you saying you're going to—?'

'I'm just ascertaining the rules in play before I decide,' he pre-empted her coolly. 'How many lovers do you take in a month?' he asked. He immediately followed up with another question purely designed to shock. 'I enjoy sex and generally have it regularly. I assume you're the same?'

Katie shut her mouth and swallowed. How could he possibly think that she'd have anywhere near the interest he had?

'The past doesn't matter,' she said briskly, fighting down the all-consuming heat this conversation was creating within her. 'There's only the future. Best not to dwell on what's gone before. I'll not be unfaithful, if that's what you'd prefer. I have no problem with celibacy.'

'Well, see…here's the thing,' he drawled with an impossibly wicked glint in his eyes. 'I don't *like* celibacy.'

'We don't need to be married long,' she said crossly. 'I'm sure six months will be long enough to…to…'

'Ensure you're left utterly undesirable?' he finished for her tartly.

'Get our business affairs straightened out.' She threw him another exasperated look.

'Six months of celibacy?' He clutched his chest and gasped theatrically, apparently appalled at the suggestion.

'Please yourself,' she retorted through gritted teeth, goaded to the extreme.

He cocked his head and that devilish smile spread over his too-perfect face. 'Is that what *you* do?'

CHAPTER TWO

ALESSANDRO KNEW HE was being outrageous, but he figured she'd asked for it by waltzing into his office and demanding not just money but his damned hand in marriage, whilst casting him as an insatiable libertine at the same time. She seemed to think he was some satyr, unable to control his voracious sexual needs.

Her 'research' had flicked his pride, and he'd been unable to resist retaliating by playing it up and making Her Total Primness here blush again. And then again.

Frankly, he'd only agreed to see her out of mild boredom. While he'd remembered her name, he hadn't remembered much else—he'd always refused to spend any time dwelling on that painful period of his past. But his commonplace curiosity had grown acute when she'd determinedly waited almost two hours to see him, and he'd turned his mind to what few memories he had of her.

She'd been a shy little thing, always hiding in the orchard and the gardens of that massive estate. Pale and too quiet. But she wasn't that quiet now Brian was trying to make her marry Carl Westin. And not now *he'd* provoked her.

She was much more interesting when provoked. In

fact she'd invigorated what had been lining up to be a tedious day facing a trillion clamouring employees, all of whom wanted a piece of him because he'd spent the last couple of weeks crisscrossing the globe as he shed a stake in one company while acquiring two others. Frankly, he'd wanted a bit of a break.

He'd figured Katie was after money and he'd been right. But her marriage proposal alongside that request had come as a complete shock.

Alessandro had crossed paths with Carl Westin a couple of years ago and the guy was a total jerk. Alessandro might party hard, but he was upfront and honest about it. He didn't cheat. Carl Westin did—in both his business and his personal life. No way was Katie Collins going to marry *him*.

But, as snappy as she might be with Alessandro, she was vulnerable to Brian's bullying.

Brian Fielding, together with his sister Naomi, had forced Alessandro out of his home. They'd taken the company that should have been his. But, most appallingly, they'd all but killed his father.

He picked up his phone, but didn't take his gaze off Katie.

'Cancel my next appointment, please, Dominique,' he instructed his assistant. 'I'm not to be disturbed.'

His interest was rooted in her absurd request, right? Nothing else. Certainly not physical attraction. From what he could see, given the boring ponytail, she had nondescript brown hair. Her eyes were a mix of green and brown and gold—he supposed they were hazel. And hidden beneath those ill-fitting ugly clothes he suspected there were some tidy curves, but not exactly generous ones.

Alessandro had been with too many women to have a particular 'type' but, even so, if he'd passed her on the street he wouldn't have given Katie Collins a second glance...

Yet there was something about her that was drawing the attention of his more basic instincts. The spark that sometimes lit her eyes, the slight pout of her soft mouth, the luminosity of her pale skin when she fired up... Yeah, it was those unexpected little flashes of spirit. He wanted to see more of them. Actually, to his total bemusement, he wanted to see her sparkle.

What he'd told her was true. He'd achieved far greater success than both Naomi and Brian had in their handling of his father's company. But Katie was more insightful than he'd acknowledged. The chance for a little revenge *was* tempting. He could buy White Oaks outright and evict them all—claim Katie's little sauce company and disband it.

If he wanted to, Alessandro could destroy everything that family owned.

That plan ought to be far more appealing than some mad idea of a mock marriage. But Katie had been desperate enough to come to him rather than run away... She really didn't feel she could. She was desperate. He'd seen it in her eyes, in the way she'd pushed past her natural reticence and snapped at him when he'd tested her. In the way she wanted to do everything she could to protect the woman she regarded as a mother...

That was a desire he did understand. That was the only thing that might actually sway him. Because once upon a time he'd wanted to do that—but he'd failed.

Grimly he shut down that line of thinking. The wound was too deep to heal and too sore to dwell on.

He focused on Katie, sitting rigidly in that chair, clutching her bag, too terrified for his conscience to handle.

'Do they know you've walked out?' he asked abruptly.

'I left a note for Susan, so she doesn't worry.'

Alessandro had always thought of Susan as the wraith of White Oaks. She was thin, and had been sort of otherworldly as she'd wandered about the vast gardens, directing operations. Brian had seduced the aging heiress, and he'd married her promising Susan everything. And yet it had come with a price. Because Brian, like his sister Naomi, had the gold-digging gene.

Alessandro's father had lost everything because of Naomi. And now it seemed Susan might lose it all because of Brian, just as her health was deteriorating to the point of complete dependence. And with Katie as her designated carer...

He wasn't seriously considering agreeing to her outlandish suggestion, was he?

But Katie's proposition had fired a reckless burn in his blood that he hadn't felt in a long time. It wasn't all about the amusement of blocking Brian...it was the prospect of sparring with Katie a little more.

'Is there no one else who can be the lucky guy?' he asked.

His question about her sexual appetite had resulted in blushing speechlessness, which in turn had tightened his skin. How innocent *was* she? Surely not completely? No woman got to her early twenties without having at least one boyfriend.

'Or am I the only one you thought of?' he prompted when she didn't immediately reply.

'I don't know anyone else to ask,' she said in a small voice. 'And not many men have your kind of money.'

He stared at her for a second and then laughed, enjoying her guileless ability to cut him down to size. 'Well, at least you're honest about why you're here.'

No sex, please—she just wanted his hard cash. And in return he'd get cold, ruthless revenge.

'We have to keep White Oaks for Susan,' she said earnestly. 'She's vulnerable.'

Once again her loyalty struck that infinitely raw spot he thought he'd buried deep.

'If you do what Brian wants and marry Carl you can keep it all,' he pointed out with ruthless precision, even though every cell rebelled at the thought of her going anywhere near that jerk.

'I shouldn't have to sacrifice the rest of my life,' she said fiercely. 'They'd expect the marriage to last. But it's *my* life. It would ruin my chances of having my own family in the future.'

Alessandro grimaced inwardly. Of course she wanted a family of her own. He couldn't think of anything worse. He had no intention of marrying and having a family. Because, much as he'd disliked her judging tone, she was right—he had plenty of options and he liked variety in his life. One woman for the rest of his days just wasn't going to happen.

'I'll work for them. I'll care for her,' she added vehemently. 'But who I marry? That's my choice.'

More memories stirred, adding to the discomfort brewing within him. He remembered those little digs at dinner. Brian always reminding her to appreciate their generosity in fostering her... Asking her wasn't she so lucky to have been chosen by them? Telling her she'd better remember that and always be grateful, because otherwise...

He realised now that Brian's underlying threat that it could all be taken away from her at any moment had been constant. He had no idea what had happened to her birth parents, but he recalled the mutinous looks she'd sometimes cast at Brian. He also remembered the pleading looks her foster mother had sent her—stopping Katie's rebellion. Keeping the peace, keeping Brian happy, had been essential to her survival.

At the time Alessandro had been too consumed by his own bitter agony of loss to think about intervening. Now he remembered it, and a lick of shame at the emotional abuse he'd witnessed burned.

He'd done nothing about it. But he'd only been a teen himself, struggling to cope with what was on his plate already. And she'd seen something of what they'd done to him, hadn't she? She knew that he'd argued with them, knew that he'd left and never looked back.

He released a tight breath, uncomfortable that she knew anything of that time. It wasn't something he ever thought about, let alone discussed. Even so, she intuitively understood that part of him still wanted to make them pay. She understood because she had that need in common—even if she'd never admit it.

Fact was, she'd been lonely and insecure most of her life. Shy, romantic, idealistic. Of course she wanted a family of her own when she was ready and met the right man. Carl Westin wasn't that man. But nor was Alessandro.

'You know what it's like to lose something—someone—you love,' she said softly. 'Won't you help to stop that from happening to me?'

Yeah, she knew a little too much about him.

'Are you trying to appeal to my generous nature now, Katie?' he asked, as idly as he could.

'I'm sure you *can* be a kind person…'

Meaning he wasn't most of the time? Her challenge sparked the desire to retaliate, and he was almost undone by the urge to haul her to her feet and into his arms. He'd show her *kind*…

The surge of desire was shocking. And wrong. She already had the unwanted attentions of one man—she didn't need them from another. He'd teased her before, but he had no intention of bullying her into anything intimate with him. No more of those jokes.

He curled his fists and shoved the inappropriate response back down deep inside. 'So, either I do this because I'm kind, and I don't want to see you suffer the same loss I did. Or I do it out of petty revenge…' He sent her a perplexed look. 'You can't have it both ways, Katie.'

'I only said that about revenge to persuade you.' She looked adorably shamefaced. 'I played it that way because you're the only person I could think of who might possibly have a reason to say yes to me.'

He sucked in a sharp breath. Yeah, she was alone and isolated. Didn't he know how that felt? And he'd had far more than her. For the first fifteen years of his life he'd had happy, loving parents…she'd never had that.

His concern for her grew when he thought of Carl Westin's reputation, of Susan's frailty, of Brian's greed…

His father hadn't been frail, but he'd been vulnerable in his own way. He'd badly wanted love. And he'd been taken advantage of just as Susan had.

Alessandro wasn't going to let Katie be forced into

marrying anyone. She needed some time out to see her way free of this puzzle. And she needed to feel in control. She obviously didn't feel that she could stand up to Brian for long Maybe Alessandro could be her temporary fix-it guy. Just not exactly in the manner she envisaged.

He straightened up decisively. 'What exactly did you have in mind? Do we announce our engagement immediately?'

Her jaw dropped. 'You're going to do it?'

'For my sins. Yeah, why not? I'll marry you.' He nodded.

She looked like a terrified deer. She sat utterly still, with her head slightly angled, as if she sensed an unseen predator, was keenly aware of the lethal danger she was in. But then she moved. She almost dived into her bag and rapidly pulled out a piece of paper covered in handwritten notes.

'I've thought it all through…'

She was suddenly a bundle of nervous energy, as if she was afraid he'd change his mind at any minute.

Of course he was going to change his mind—but she didn't need to know that yet.

'I imagine you've thought of everything…' he muttered.

'I didn't sleep well last night, and I had all the train journey to finish researching.' She was so engrossed in her explanation she didn't even seem to notice his sarcasm.

'What's the plan?'

'Las Vegas.'

He stared at her. 'In America?'

'Yes.' She smiled brightly, as if he were a bit dim.

'That's the one. If we have our paperwork with us then it can be very quick. There's an all-in-one hotel and chapel venue. It's open all hours.'

Wow. She made it sound unmissable. And so urgent.

'I imagine you do have your paperwork with you?'

'I do.' She nodded. 'There's a flight later this afternoon. Nonstop. We could catch it...' She petered out as she saw the distaste on his face.

'Are you talking about a commercial flight?' he asked.

'Um...yes.' She stared at him.

'You want me to drop everything and leave *now*?'

Was she really that desperate to escape Brian?

'Would that be okay?' She fiddled with the strap on her horrible fake leather bag. 'We can be there and back in just a few days. I'll be gone less than a week. The sooner it's done...'

She paled as she looked at the screen of the tablet on his desk, and then colour rushed into her cheeks so quickly he wondered if she were unwell.

His entire body tensed. 'Are you that afraid of him, Katie?'

She hesitated. 'I'm afraid I won't be able to say no to him for ever.'

'But you *can* say no to me?' He really shouldn't feel as if that were a challenge.

She nodded a little too vigorously. 'You have no reason to ask anything of me. I'm the last person a guy like you would want in his life. I'm no risk to you and you're no risk to me.'

Instinct argued against that instantly. In fact, he wasn't sure he'd heard a *less* true statement. That feeling was crazy...she was no threat to his business, his career, anything. Yet his sixth sense still warned him.

Did he really want to revisit the miseries of his past when he'd come so far? Would the Fielding siblings come after him?

Bring it on.

'Once it's all arranged with you—once we're married—then I'll get straight back and look after Susan.'

He checked at that comment and shot her a measuring glance. For Katie to spend her early twenties nursing her foster mother round the clock wasn't healthy. She needed her own life, her own career. But he wasn't about to go there—not yet. One issue at a time.

'It'll only be for a few months…to ensure Brian doesn't try anything else,' Katie continued in that rushed fashion. 'You'll get a stake in my sauce company, and you'll get the property in the end—we just give Susan lifelong residency rights. You won't lose any money…'

He waved away her breathy, too-earnest promises.

Katie Collins was in trouble. She just couldn't see another way out of it. If he were to get her out of the country and away from Brian the bully for a while she'd have time to clear her head and see sense. He'd think up a better plan when he was more refreshed too.

'I'm not going on a commercial flight.'

He checked his watch and made a few calculations. He could catch up on some work away from the constant interruptions in the office. She'd get the rest she clearly needed. They'd resolve it easily from there.

'But we can still go today, seeing as you're that impatient.'

'We can?'

Her eyes shone, their amber centres flickering like

fire. Her lips parted, reddened and soft, and her skin simply glowed. She was luminescent. Sparkling wasn't the word—she was suddenly stunning.

Alessandro's skin tightened. Suddenly he wanted to get closer and *taste*.

'Thank you so much. I really appreciate your help.'

She sent him a huge smile of gratitude. As if he was some kindly uncle. Alessandro leaned closer, feeling that frisson of danger—of something forbidden—sharpen.

'Don't start thinking I'm *kind*, Katie,' he muttered without thinking. 'Because I'm not. I'm ambitious and I'm always out for myself. Everything I do stems from selfish motivations, so rest assured I'll claim complete payment for this.'

Her smile froze. 'Of course,' she breathed nervously. 'Whatever you want…all you have to do is ask.'

CHAPTER THREE

ALESSANDRO STARED, FLOORED by the husky innocence of her reply. He just needed to ask? He ground back the inappropriate, obvious response. Why was he degenerating into some lame jerk who took every chance to turn the conversation towards the sexual? Why was he thinking of sex at all around her? He refused to be no better than the bastard prospective fiancé she was escaping—full of unwanted amorous attention...

But at the same time Alessandro had never met a woman he couldn't seduce. That wasn't to say he'd slept with every woman he'd met, and he was hardly about to seduce Katie. That would be like a lion playing with a lamb. Disastrous for her and unsatisfying for him.

But as he studied her closer he discovered more— her delicate chin, her high cheekbones—and then he returned to her complex coloured eyes that changed with the light, or perhaps with her mood. Elfin-featured, fine-boned...she was stunning when he teased that worry from her eyes and replaced it with excitement.

And she was as aware of him as he was of her. He needed very little of his vast experience to know that.

Temptation tugged.

No.

He whirled away from her fascinating features, dismissing those wayward thoughts, and picked up his phone again instead.

'Dominique, I need a report on Brian and Susan Fielding, owners of White Oaks Hall—business dealings as well as personal. I also need a complete update on Zetticci Foods. Latest financials, forecasts, reviews, analysis, new product offerings from the last couple of years, plus their performance and internal management structure. The same with any company Carl Westin is involved with. I want *everything*. Email it ASAP.'

He needed information and ammunition.

'I also need the jet ready to leave for the States in an hour. Cancel all my meetings for the next...' He mulled for a moment and factored in the travel time. 'Five days.'

As always Dominique simply said yes, and Alessandro hung up.

'I need your passport.' He gestured to Katie, who was sitting with her mouth ajar. 'For the flight manifest, border control conditions and so on.' He waggled his fingers impatiently.

Katie snapped her mouth shut, wordlessly rummaged in her bag and handed the document to him. As he strode out to give it to Dominique he quickly flicked through it. None of the pages was stamped—which didn't mean she'd hadn't travelled, at least within Europe—but it looked almost brand-new. His curiosity sharpened.

Back in his office, she was still clutching the bag like it was some kind of protective shield.

'Did you leave your suitcase out in Reception?' he asked.

'I...uh...no.' She shook her head.

'You don't have any clothes with you?'

Her eyes widened.

He bit back another laugh, refusing to verbalise the next obvious innuendo.

'Not even a toothbrush?' A hit of pleasure warmed his blood at the prospect of getting her out of that plain skirt and into something that fitted her better. 'It doesn't matter. We'll get you something over there.'

He had five days—an eternity in his usual high-speed schedule. This was a chance to lay old ghosts to rest and to enjoy a mild distraction. Hell, in five days he could easily seduce her into surrender—not complete, of course, just enough to soothe the irritation she'd inflicted on him. She might think he was a shameless playboy, but for all her protests she was not immune.

He smiled to himself. The satisfaction of her acknowledging *that* was going to be good.

All of which proved he'd been working too hard lately. It was past time for some play.

It was all happening so much faster than Katie had imagined—though frankly she hadn't imagined any further than getting into his office, let alone actually convincing him to go to Vegas with her.

But *not* for five days. That was far too long to leave Susan. They needed to fly over today and back tomorrow. She'd suggest that to him a little later, though. She didn't want to say anything that might make him change his mind before they were married.

Nervously she accompanied him to the basement, where a car and driver waited. A few moments later they were on the road to City Airport.

Alessandro took calls for the entire journey. In the

majority of them he spoke in Italian, meaning that Katie didn't understand a word, but his urbane, confident tones slipped beneath her skin, stirring a secret response she couldn't bear to acknowledge.

She stared fixedly out of the window, trying to minimise his impact on her senses. He was too handsome, too powerful, too full of wicked humour that made her want to smile all the time.

And he'd agreed to go with her to Vegas.

Get a grip.

But the knots tightened in her stomach as they arrived at the airport.

Another assistant was waiting at the entrance to the private jet terminal and he handed Alessandro a folder of paperwork and a large paper bag. As they walked through the building Alessandro showed her the Sybarite deli logo stamped on the side.

'I'm looking forward to tasting your work.' His lips twitched and he leaned closer. 'Lots of things you can do with sauce…sharpen up even the blandest of dishes, correct?'

She sent him a death look.

He laughed. 'You're easy to bait, Katie.'

Breathless, she failed to think of a reply. Why did she keep reading innuendo into everything he said?

Because he means you to.

He was an outrageous tease. While he'd been intimidating when she'd first arrived in his office, it hadn't taken long till he'd flipped the switch to a playful side that was his natural, wicked self. It wasn't actually anything to do with *her*. Except she kept overreacting.

She had to keep her response in check and not take him seriously—that would be no problem at all, right?

All her life she'd played it safe—almost always backing down from causing a scene even when she'd wanted to, rarely disobeying Brian, never fighting back because Susan had been so anxious the few times she had. She'd invariably stayed within the rules her authoritarian foster father had set.

But Alessandro barely seemed to bother with rules at all.

'You own this?' she muttered as they swiftly walked through the terminal and onto the tarmac. To her ignorant eyes the immaculate plane looked brand-new.

'I own a stake in a jet leasing company. Better for the environmental footprint if we share the private planes around a bit.'

He laughed at her withering look of disbelief.

Yes, Alessandro Zetticci had interests in as many companies as he had in women. Fiendishly energetic and astute, he had a knack for knowing what people wanted, what they liked, before they were even aware of it.

She knew he'd used that innate sophistication as a youth and set up his first venue. It had rapidly become the ultimate nightspot for high society, celebrities, models, wannabes... Then at the height of its popularity he'd sold it, taken the stellar profits and reinvested them into a new company—again using that innate foresight.

He created and then flicked on companies with the careless ease with which he traded women. From one company to the next, amassing a property portfolio and personal fortune at the same time.

'What?' Alessandro prompted as she paused to look up at the plane again.

'It's bigger than I expected.'

It seemed massive for just the two of them.

That smile hovered on his lips. 'Oh?'

She shot him another death look. 'Do you put sexual innuendo into *all* of your conversations?'

'As much as I can, of course,' he drawled, the wickedness in his smile deepening. 'Being the lascivious playboy that I am.'

'You're only doing it to antagonise me now,' she said.

'Am I?'

'Or you're just practising your flirty banter. Which you don't need to.'

'Don't I?' A flicker of astonishment lit his eyes. 'Why not?'

No man had ever spoken to her this way, and she'd certainly never answered back. But with a man like Alessandro offence was the best defence, wasn't it? Surely she should fight fire with fire?

She glared at him. 'Any woman with eyes would say yes to you. You don't even have to open your mouth.'

He burst out laughing—all warmth and wicked energy. 'But a closed mouth isn't as good, Katie.' He chuckled again and teased her. 'Don't you want to know what my tongue is *really* good at?'

Refusing to reply, she stomped up the stairs. She was still unable to believe he'd agreed to marry her. But that was him, right? Mercurial, maverick, mischievous. This must appeal to that renegade element within him that enjoyed wild, spontaneous adventures. Indeed, she heard him chuckle again close behind her.

'You react so prudishly, how am I supposed to resist?' he murmured.

She turned her head, taking the chance to look down

on him for once. 'You could just try being polite instead of trying to embarrass me.'

He sent her a fake wounded look. 'But, Katie, I'm unfailingly polite.'

She knew he didn't mean it. He was still laughing at her. She had the horrible feeling he knew she was too aware of him. Somehow she needed to keep him at a distance.

At the top of the stairs she shyly followed a uniformed crewman through to the main passenger section of the plane. She drew in a deep breath because it was stunning—luxury leather, gleaming chrome, plush carpet and an outrageous sense of space.

The crewman demonstrated how the extra-wide seats reclined and pointed out the stack of reading material stowed in a gorgeous side table with a glossy finish. Then he showed her a partition further down the back of the plane, beyond which was a beautiful linen-clad bed and a polished bathroom facility. It was pure decadent elegance.

'Thank you,' she murmured as the crewman disappeared back the way he'd come.

'We have three pilots and one assistant for a flight of this duration,' Alessandro explained as he put his folders, bag and tablet down. 'If there's anything you need just ask and it will be done.'

Three pilots? Some oxygen might be good right now.

'Where are they?' she asked.

'Crew quarters.' He sat in the seat opposite the one she'd taken and smiled as she fumbled with the seatbelt. 'Are you okay?'

'I haven't travelled that much,' she confessed with an embarrassed smile.

His eyes narrowed. 'You've flown before, though, right?'

'I went to Paris on a school trip, but we went on the train.'

'You've never flown at *all*?' he queried keenly, but then he smiled, and it was that wicked one. 'Well, it's always good to begin with the best. Start as you mean to go on, *si*?'

This was definitely the best. And Katie couldn't quite contain her smile as she leaned back and looked out of the window as the plane taxied to the end of the runway.

'You're not scared?' Alessandro asked, watching her curiously.

She shook her head, determinedly keeping her attention on the window as they took off. The view of the city was incredible. 'It's amazing...' she breathed.

After a few minutes she glanced back at Alessandro, absurdly disappointed to see him engrossed in reading something on his tablet. She watched quietly as he swiped through page after page. His frown deepened as he took notes with the pen and notepad he'd balanced skilfully on his knee.

He might be a playboy, but he also knew how to work. That was what those 'most eligible bachelor' articles gushed about—not just his legendary woman-slaying status, but his second-to-none work ethic. He had to be driven to have achieved the success he had in only ten years. How had he managed it? Intelligent, determined, decisive...known for his deals...he was always ahead of everyone else.

She just didn't want him to change his mind. So she sat silently, trying to blend into the background the way she did when Brian was in one of his moods. But she felt hot and uncomfortable, ridiculously aware of that bed behind her.

No doubt Alessandro would bring women on flights with him all the time—hit that mile-high club time after time in complete comfort. The crew certainly hadn't batted any eyelids when they'd seen her with him. Who knew how many women he'd had in there? It was a den of debauchery.

'You don't want to lie down and rest for a while?' He suddenly glanced up and seemed to pick up on the direction of her thoughts. 'You've had a long day of travelling already.'

'No, thanks,' she answered immediately, her skin burning at the thought. 'I'm fine.'

As he held her gaze his expression turned wickedly quizzical. 'What are you thinking about Katie?'

'Nothing,' she lied.

'So "nothing" makes you blush like that?'

Katie pointedly turned away and buried her nose in the nearest magazine.

Alessandro huffed out a tight breath. He was trying to keep his temper in check, but the reports Dominique had emailed over just before their departure were making it impossible. Brian Fielding might be hyper-controlling over his wife and Katie, but he was very much out of control in his own life. He was one of those jerks who thought he could have it all without doing any work— gambling not only with cards and chance machines, but with get-rich-quick schemes and insecure investments. One of which, ironically, was Zetticci Foods.

His father's former company was in worse shape than Alessandro had realised. While Aldo had been a creative genius—an instinctive, outstanding chef, with innate knowledge and a passion for his work—since his death the company's direction had faltered.

As CEO, Naomi had clearly gone for a splatter gun approach, throwing out a ton of new products and hoping one would hit the market. None had. She'd sacked every one of the chefs she'd brought on board over the years and then turned to her brother Brian for a cash injection.

And what Brian had told Katie was correct. They were on the brink of losing White Oaks, Susan's home and inheritance. According to the brief report, the older woman was now wheelchair-bound and being cared for by family at home. Being cared for by *Katie*—because Brian was regularly travelling to conferences, active on local government board meetings…

Alessandro grimaced. Brian was all about the show.

He glanced up from the report, his gaze unerringly landing on Katie again. When she'd mentioned her sauces earlier she'd lit up enough to nudge his curiosity. He'd got an assistant to track down a sample from that deli and bring it to the airport.

'Are you hungry?' he asked.

She sent him a startled look, then swiftly averted her gaze. He watched with mild incredulity as yet another blush washed over her skin.

'Katie,' he mocked in a low voice, '*you're* the one reading innuendo into everything I say.'

He had to admit he found it both amusing and arousing. The fact that she was so aware of him was a kind of balm—because her effect on *him* wasn't just arousing, it was irritating.

'It's the way you look when you say it,' she grumbled, glancing back to shoot him daggers yet again.

Hugely entertained, he cocked his head and muttered coyly, 'Oh, I forgot…it's my looks…'

'You have no idea what it's like for us mere mortals,' she ground out.

She didn't think herself attractive? He arched his eyebrows at her and waited.

'We're invisible,' she explained when she finally got sick of his silence.

The last thing she'd been to him all day was *invisible*. The more she opened her mouth, the more he was fascinated by what she had to say and by the sweetness of the lips doing the speaking. They looked so lush, and here he was wondering if other parts of her were as perfect…

He was so tempted, so curious to taste and explore, that somehow he'd become every inch the satyr she'd pegged him as. Every thought was related to her being naked and sprawled on a bed before him. Which, contrary to popular opinion, was *not* the way he usually worked. He enjoyed women—always—but he could take it or leave it. He'd never felt desire as if it were an addiction before.

'You know you have power over people,' she added.

'Are you treating me like a piece of meat, Katie?' he muttered, acutely aware of the irony in his accusation. 'Are you sure it's only my looks? What about my money? My charm? My extraordinary intelligence?'

'Let's not forget your outsize ego.'

'Yet you're defining me only by my appearance,' he mocked.

She pressed her lips together. He wished she wouldn't bite back her snap.

'Are you treating me like a toy, Alessandro?' She glared at him. 'Am I here for your amusement? To liven up an otherwise boring day?'

She was so on the mark that he nearly winced. Instead he leaned back in his seat, irritated by his uncontrollable inappropriate thinking and her superficial judgement. Why should he care what she thought of him?

'Is that what women are for you?' she added softly.

'Do you want me to marry you or not?' he growled.

She seemed to freeze. Then she pulled on a tight smile. 'Are *you* hungry?' she enquired, very politely.

He suddenly felt sorry, because he'd scared her into compliance—he'd not meant to, but he'd threatened to take away what she wanted. In that moment he was no better than Brian.

'Always,' he grumbled—and he meant no innuendo in that.

Frankly, he often forgot to eat when he was working flat-out, and he'd been working around the clock these last couple of weeks to pull together some deals. So, come to think of it, he did have a mighty hollow deep in his belly.

She looked down at the table between them and then glanced back up at him. 'Do you want to try my sauces?' she asked.

Her voice sounded huskier than usual, and it was his turn to shoot her a look.

'Really?' He began to laugh, because that had been such a cute little tease. 'Not bad!'

To his delight, she suddenly laughed too. And she was gorgeous doing it.

'Sorry...' she murmured once she'd recovered her equilibrium.

No. He didn't want her ever to be sorry for giving as good as she got. She was prickly, quick to repel any possible suggestion of something between them. But there was something, and now she'd put the image in his head of licking some luscious sauce off her naked flesh. The blast of heat in his body was beyond uncomfortable.

Purely for something to do to distract himself, he lifted four small bottles out of the brown paper bag he'd stashed beside him.

'Nice packaging,' he noted. They looked more professional than he'd expected, with their simple green and white labels. 'Which should I try first?'

She shrugged her shoulders.

He fetched a few small plates from the galley and poured a little from each bottle onto them.

'You don't want a cracker or something to put it on?' she asked.

Or something.

He inwardly growled at his one-track lustathon thinking—had he regressed a few millennia to become some hormone-overloaded caveman? He'd last been with a beautiful woman only a few weeks ago, before work had ramped up so much. It wasn't as if he'd had a dry spell...*ever.*

It's because she said she didn't want you.

His pride was pricked. He hated being told he couldn't do something. Authority issues from the bad days of his late teens, he mocked himself. Being denied something made him all the more determined to do—to take or have—whatever it was he'd been banned from. So, yes, naturally he now wanted to *do* Ms Katie

Collins. He wanted it more with every passing minute. But he couldn't be that jerk—she had enough of those in her life already.

Focus on the food.

He tried the apricot sauce first. It punched his taste-buds so hard he closed his eyes, inhaling sharply at the intensity. This was better than good.

He blinked and stared at her accusingly. 'You made this?'

'Well, I have help to pick the fruit—' She broke off warily and coloured.

Diverted, he wondered who helped her with the fruit picking.

But then she continued, 'And I use the kitchen in the house.'

She literally made them all herself? 'Whose recipes?'

'My own.' She sat a little straighter. 'I'm quite good at it… Though really it's the herbs. We grow those too.'

'You have your very own special blend of herbs and spices?' he drawled.

'Is that so hard to believe?' she asked with a little reproach.

He cleared his throat. 'You've done some culinary courses?'

That flush in her cheeks resurged. 'I tried to do a couple of courses at the local institute, but I couldn't leave Susan. So I learned from every cooking channel I could find.'

She tilted her chin with prim defensiveness, daring him to question her. Her eyes glinted, filling with quiet confidence in the face of his surprise.

'What else do you have aside from these?' he asked, trying to steady his appetite.

'Don't you like them?' she asked, looking as if butter wouldn't melt in her mouth.

'You don't need my feedback,' he said roughly. 'You know damn well how delicious they are.'

Her smile blossomed, igniting a glow that seemed fuelled by something deep within her. 'I *know*, right?' She laughed cheekily.

His gut tightened at her unexpected confidence. Coy little trickster... It turned out that she, like her sauce, was passionate, confident and full of sassy flavour. At least in regard to this. The turnaround from the wet lamb who'd wandered into his office on wobbly legs only a couple of hours ago was astounding. In this moment—in this one thing—she shone.

'Like I said, I use the fruit we grow.' She reached forward, turning the bottles so the labels faced her. 'Those apricots are a heritage variety. Same with the plums.'

Alessandro nodded, slightly dazed. He'd never found discussing fruit trees fascinating before, but he couldn't take his eyes from her. He thought again that she was like her sauces—intense, fiery and sweet.

'Susan's father planted those trees,' she added softly. 'I help her care for them, cook their fruit. I love it.'

And that love came out in the flavour of her creations.

Unsettling long-ignored memories stirred. His father had been like that—guided by instinct and emotion. Alessandro had always been more interested in the business side of things. His analytical brain worked better in bigger picture ways. Katie was self-taught and humble, and she had inimitable warmth.

Another searing shaft of hunger strained his resolve. The desire to touch her almost derailed his reason. As she blossomed before him he ached to conquer and claim…

A horrible thought occurred to him. Had hideous Carl Westin ever seen her like this?

'Maybe this is what he wants,' he muttered, before thinking better of it.

She sent him a mystified look. 'Who?'

He blinked. 'Carl. Your sauces.'

Her jaw dropped as she stared at him in astonishment. 'You think he wants my recipes?'

No. He did not. But the fact that she honestly believed he might showed just how oblivious to her own beauty she was. Alessandro half laughed, even as he was almost overcome by the urge to haul her out of that seat.

He could have her soft, yielding sweetness beneath him in an instant. He'd discover her true taste. But he swallowed the desire back.

He forced his focus back to the sauces. 'Which is your favourite?'

'The cherry vinegar.' She dipped her finger into the small pool he'd poured onto the plate and sucked the sauce off the tip of it.

Any other woman he'd have thought was making a deliberately seductive move, but there was too much of the innocent in Katie's eyes.

To his total torment, she'd left a tiny smear just above her lip. At that sight all his good intentions melted. He couldn't resist that contrary look in her eyes. Like the myriad of colours it was all reflected there—confidence, caution, humour, haughtiness…and desire. It was beyond temptation.

'Alessandro?' She sat very still as he swiftly rose from his seat. 'What are you doing?'

'Tasting the cherry.'

He braced his hands on the armrests of her seat and slowly bent closer. Hesitating, testing, allowing her the space, the time, to pull away, to say something. She didn't. Pleasure washed over him and he hadn't even touched her. He gently licked that little smear from her mouth. At the tiny hitch in her breathing he brushed his lips that bit lower, to cover hers.

He'd steal only the lightest, quickest of kisses. A tiny tease…just *because*. She expected it anyway, didn't she? He couldn't let her down, what with all her wild assumptions about him.

'Katie?' he asked, searching.

She stayed still and silent, but the expression in her eyes said it all.

There was a moment, the tiniest of pauses, when his lips were barely pressed against hers at all, and then he returned with a gorgeous, luscious pressure that simply melted Katie. His tongue traced over her lips in a teasing slide until she opened and let him in.

This was a kiss.

This was everything all in one soft touch. In mere moments her heart pounded, suddenly too big for her chest, as he stole—and gave—an experience like no other.

He sparked something within her. A trickle that ran faster, fuller, until it became an intense warmth, flooding her system. She strained closer to let herself taste him the way he was tasting her. He deepened the contact, swirling his tongue into her hungry mouth, and shyly, eagerly, instinctively she matched him.

The dizzying sensation intensified. Delight mixed

with heat and an ache for more. She shivered, seeking his touch on her skin. She wanted to get closer and she didn't want this to stop. It was too nice. She'd never experienced anything so nice.

Suddenly she was seized with the conviction that nothing was ever going to be the same. *She* was never going to be the same. He'd awakened a need so intense she thought it could never be met. And in that moment of realisation—of shocking recognition and burgeoning desire, of undeniable deep need—she moaned.

He suddenly lifted himself away and stepped back.

Katie pressed herself into her seat, desperately putting more distance between them as she tried to recover her breath. She gazed up, dying inside when she registered his casual expression. Why wasn't he breathless?

'You can't… You shouldn't…' She trailed off, unable to scramble a sentence together. Why wasn't he shattered?

It was just a kiss. You're taking it too seriously.

That amused look in his eyes grew as she struggled to regain her sensibility.

'That wasn't fair,' she breathed.

'Not fair?' He returned to his seat and folded his arms across his chest.

'You were only supposed to sample my sauces.'

Instead they'd both discovered he could seduce her with a snap of his fingers. Her flush burned.

'Oh, yes, the sauces,' he echoed with soft irony. 'You really created them all by yourself?'

'Why is that so hard to believe?' she snapped balefully. 'You don't think I can be good at anything?'

'I think we've both just figured out what you're good at.'

She gaped, flummoxed into speechlessness, and felt that wretched burn of embarrassment slide over her skin again. He was so skilled, so charming…no wonder all those women fell into his bed.

Now he smiled at her wickedly. 'If you don't want me to kiss you again, then stop fishing for compliments.'

Her jaw fell open. Was she meant to be *grateful* for his kisses? 'I don't need you to kiss me to make me feel better about myself.'

He reached forward to the plates on the table, swirled his finger in the cherry vinegar sauce and licked it off with a lascivious flourish. 'No, you just need me to marry you to help you escape your evil guardian.'

He made it sound ridiculous. As if *she* was being ridiculous. But she could see no other way to keep White Oaks safe for Susan.

'Yes,' she ground out through gritted teeth. 'And that's *all* I want from you.'

CHAPTER FOUR

BACK IN LONDON it would be almost midnight, but here in Las Vegas it was early evening. Not that there was any sense of time in this city. It was always open...always ready to entertain. And the last thing Alessandro wanted right now was to find himself anywhere near a bedroom with Katie Collins.

He never should have kissed her.

Gritting his teeth, Alessandro guided her through customs clearance and then straight into the limo his assistant had organised.

Their hotel was on the main strip, suitably ritzy and fantastically distracting, with ornate decor and vast, gleaming lounge areas. The receptionist handed him a key card while the porters took his luggage. Of course Katie didn't have any.

He turned and looked at her, standing in the centre of the luxurious lobby. The wide-eyed amazement on her pretty face was priceless.

He never, ever should have kissed her.

He tensed as desire rippled through his body. Pushing it down, he glanced away and rubbed his hand over his face. He was tired, *si*? Hence the loss of self-control. But he'd pull himself together. They'd take in the view, have dinner, have a rational and realistic chat about Katie's future...

Except he didn't think he could actually be alone with her yet. Not after the sensual torture of the plane trip. His awareness of her was shocking, and he was unaccustomed to travelling with a woman like this—to being close, but not being able to touch her more than that kiss he'd already stolen.

A massive mistake.

Maybe once Susan was settled and Katie was away from the horror foster father Alessandro could indulge in a liaison with her, but until then it was too complicated.

'Do you want to head up to the suite or shall we take a look around first?' He offered her the choice to check how she was feeling.

She eagerly accepted the safe option. 'Let's look around.'

He grimaced wryly. Yeah, she didn't want to be alone with him. To her he was the big, bad wolf. And she was right to be wary. He did want to eat her. He'd pounce the second she suggested it.

Instead he followed her into the bar, abandoning any idea of a rational discussion until morning. They were both too tired and tense. Having a moment to lighten up would be good for them. But there was no reason why he couldn't keep teasing her—just a little. To deny himself that last little pleasure with her would be a step too far, and Alessandro wasn't accustomed to self-denial.

The bar was three-quarters full already—people were out to enjoy themselves in all the ways they could in this town.

'Look at the colours in that cocktail.' Katie's colourful eyes gleamed as they passed a table full of laughing women. 'It's beautiful.'

She sounded almost wistful as they took their seats in an intimate alcove with a view across the bar.

'You don't want to know what's in it?' Alessandro asked dryly, sinking into a seat that he knew was going to be far too comfortable.

'Something that beautiful is bound to taste good, don't you think?' she smiled.

Her words struck home if he applied them to *her*. 'You can have one,' he growled.

Her gaze widened, then narrowed. 'I asked you to marry me—not turn into my mother.'

The temptation to kiss her almost overwhelmed him and he grasped for self-control. 'When did you last have an alcoholic drink?'

Her chin lifted higher and a mutinous look sharpened her eyes. But she didn't reply.

Yeah, she'd never drunk alcohol...she'd never travelled. What else had she never done? Because there'd been inexperience in her kiss. Sweet, shy, hot, totally tempting inexperience.

There'd also been a burst of fire.

'One,' he reiterated unapologetically, and nodded to the waiter. Neither of them needed anything to fan the flames.

The waiter returned shortly, bearing a tray with the most outrageous cocktail Alessandro had ever seen. Given that he'd spent a large chunk of his adult life building hospitality venues, he'd pretty much seen every cocktail there was. This one featured bright green and orange layers of pure alcohol and vaguely resembled a vibrant parrot. Too late he realised that if Katie were to have more than two mouthfuls things might veer off course.

'I'm not sure that—'

Too late. She'd already sipped.

'Oh…' She swallowed and sucked in a breath. Surprise widened her eyes. 'It's even more delicious than I imagined.'

Was this a thirst to drown her sorrows? Or cool her down?

Alessandro swiftly reached across and picked up her glass before she had the chance to lift it again. He was saving her from herself, he thought morosely. He swallowed the vile sweet liquid with an appalled grimace.

'Whisky, please,' he wheezed to the waiter, who hadn't had a chance to get more than five feet away. 'Double.'

'You didn't like it?' Katie enquired meekly, but that tiny twinkle in her eyes gave her away.

He laughed, enjoying her flash of attitude. It was so much better than that cowed, fearful look he'd seen on her in his office. Now she had some sparkle.

'You know I didn't.'

He watched as she pushed back the sleeves of her schoolgirlish white blouse. He glanced around at the glittering interior of the bar and sternly told himself not to stare at the tiny amount of skin the action exposed. Since when was he fascinated by less than a square inch of skin? When his dates usually wore so much less?

Alessandro took a sip as soon as his whisky arrived, and cursed his inner devil who'd thought this was a good idea. Desperate for distraction, he pulled out his phone and realised he'd neglected to switch it on after the flight. He frowned as multiple messages from Dominque pinged. All asking him to call her urgently.

Before he could, the phone buzzed in his hand.

'What is it?' he asked tersely. Dominique wouldn't bother him unless it was important.

'Alessandro, I've been trying to get hold of you.' Dominque sounded concerned. 'Something's come up in our research on White Oaks,' she continued crisply. 'Katie Collins's engagement to Carl Westin was announced in the papers today.'

'Pardon?' He stilled, unsure he'd heard correctly.

He glanced at Katie. She was watching him, her hand tightening around her lurid drink, her eyes widening with fear as microseconds passed.

'Katie's engagement,' Dominique repeated. 'It only went online an hour ago—that's why I missed it earlier.'

'Where?'

Dominique told him the newspaper's name.

'I'll call you back,' he said briskly.

He reached out and took the glass from Katie's hand.

'What's wrong?' Her voice sounded thin and shadows had dimmed that earlier sparkle.

'Have you checked your phone for messages?'

She rummaged in her bag and hauled out her phone. 'Is it Susan?' Tears sprang to her eyes. 'I shouldn't have left her. Not even for a day.'

She was actually shaking, and as she fumbled with her phone she dropped it.

'It's not Susan,' he said quietly, scooping up the phone from the floor for her. 'Breathe.' His chest tightened at the concern in her expression. 'It appears that your engagement to Carl was announced this afternoon.'

'That's not possible.' Katie froze, her shocked gaze fixed on him. 'I didn't agree. I said no. I'd *never* agree.'

Yeah, Little Miss Bigamist she was not—but Brian had gone ahead and announced it anyway.

'He can't actually make me, can he?' She snatched her phone from him and switched it on. 'I've got lots of missed calls.' She stared at it in horror. 'Brian, mostly.' She paled even more as she held the phone to her ear.

He could hear the berating tone of Brian's message even from across the table. And he could also hear Katie's breathing quicken.

His own anger pounded in his ears. Brian the bully was ramping up the attack, telling her the engagement was now public knowledge so she couldn't bring shame on the family, couldn't embarrass Susan. Susan who'd gone to bed, so distressed that Katie had left…

Alessandro reached out and took the phone from Katie, turning it off before tossing it onto the table between them. He rubbed his forehead, struggling to think clearly. He regretted the long flight and that one whisky, and all the hours in the last fortnight during which he'd worked and not slept. But he had to do something— anything to help ease Katie's anxiety.

The obvious solution stared him in the face. They'd come this far so they might as well complete the picture. Right now it felt like the fastest, easiest option. The decision was easy.

He'd be the villain of the piece. The scoundrel who had seduced some other man's fiancée away from him…

With the added scandalous frisson of the family connection between them, people were going to love the gossip. But Alessandro didn't care about his own reputation. Right now all he cared about was clearing the panic from Katie's face and stopping Brian from browbeating her into something she didn't want.

They'd forced him out all those years ago, but Alessandro had his own resources now, and he had no one else to worry about. Katie had Susan, and without some extra support she'd be trapped.

'Should I call him back?' Katie asked in a horrified whisper.

'No,' he growled, but then softened his tone. Brian's greed was coming to an end. 'Not yet.'

She swayed a little as she stood. He put his hands on her shoulders to steady her and looked into her eyes.

'You came to me for help, Katie. That's what you want, right?' he asked.

'I want to know that Susan—'

'I'll ensure she's okay. Trust me.'

The sooner Katie was tied to him, the more freedom he'd have to act on her behalf.

She stared up at him, the myriad of colours in her eyes reflecting a myriad of conflicting emotions—fear, mostly, but also hope, and a last hint of awareness.

'Are you sure, Katie?' he asked harshly. 'You really want to do this?'

She looked exhausted and terrified and too damn trusting. All he wanted was her smile and those flashing little sparks in her eyes to come back.

She nodded. 'Yes. Please.'

Katie stood still, her face cupped in strong but gentle hands. The lips moving over hers were warm and assured and teasing, sending flickers of temptation along her veins, stirring the yearning that ran so deep.

She moaned, her lips parting, seeking the slide of his tongue. She liked it when he— *Yes...* The trickle of sensation became a torrent within her and she moaned again. *Like that.* She liked it when he kissed her like that. Deep and gentle and powerful.

'Katie...'

'Mmm?'

The whisper confused her. How could he whisper her name like that while he was kissing her so passionately at the exact same time?

'Katie?'

She breathed in deeply, not wanting to move, floating in a cocoon of warmth, relaxed and happy. She slowly blinked, opened her eyes and smiled.

And then immediately froze.

Reality rushed in on her with sickening speed. She wasn't being kissed in some dream world. She was in bed and she wasn't alone.

Alessandro Zetticci was only inches away, lying facing her, his head propped on his hand. There was an odd expression in his eyes.

'You were moaning,' he said, watching her too closely.

She couldn't reply. Was he *naked*? The part of him she could see above the sheet covering them was naked. There was a vast expanse of bronzed, muscular torso on show.

Katie stared. She couldn't breathe. Couldn't move. Couldn't speak.

'Katie?'

'What are you doing in here?'

He blinked and that wicked smile widened. 'Should I leave?' He pushed down the sheet.

'No!' Huge mistake. *Huge.* Oh. *So* huge.

The man just had everything, didn't he? Long, powerful limbs. Long, powerful... Well, *everything.*

She hurriedly tugged the sheet back up to cover him. 'You're not wearing anything.'

He stared at her for a second and then seemed to take in a steadying breath.

'Actually, I'm not *quite* naked,' he corrected her. 'I kept my boxers on—which is kind of me, given I don't like underwear.'

'Of course you don't,' she muttered desperately, wondering how on earth they'd—

'I get a rash from cheap synthetic fabrics,' he offered in explanation, but wicked humour danced in his eyes.

'Are you sure it's from the fabric?' she snapped back before she could think.

He laughed as he rubbed a hand through his sinfully sexy, slightly-too-long-to-be-good hair. 'I knew the kitten had claws...' He drew in a deep breath and stretched out.

'I'm not a kitten. But I *am* devastated to discover you're not perfect.'

'I never said I was perfect—that was your assumption.' He grinned at her. 'I prefer cotton, or silk—or, better yet, nothing at all.' His eyes glinted.

He was a naturist? Wonderful.

They'd been in *bed* together. Of course it was nothing to him to get into bed with a woman—he did it all the time. But *she* didn't. He was the most masculine thing ever to have graced her bed. Okay, he was the *only* thing ever to have graced her bed.

She swallowed as she remembered the madness of the night before.

'Did we...?' She trailed off, still distracted by all the skin he had on show.

His gaze narrowed on her. 'Do you not remember?'

Her brain was too fried by the sight of him in all his near nude glory to remember her own name, let alone much else.

'Did we—?'

'Sleep together? Sure.' His eyebrows lifted. 'Katie,' he said, as if lecturing an imbecile, 'if we'd done anything *more* you wouldn't need to ask. Your virtue is safe.'

Yeah, she'd figured that. Because while he might be all but naked she was still completely dressed. Her blouse, skirt, bra, panties…everything. But she was still mortified—*so* mortified.

'We got married,' she whispered.

He stilled and his teasing smile froze. 'Yes, we did.'

She closed her eyes. She ought to feel relief. Wasn't that what she'd wanted? Only all she could feel was *heat*.

That dream she'd been having was a memory, and she'd been reliving it. Her brain had picked the highlight to replay. Not those phone messages from Brian, nor that engagement announcement, nor Alessandro's rapid, decisive response. Not even the fact that he'd marched her off and married her in less than an hour. All she could think about was the kiss that had sealed the deal.

'Here.'

She opened her eyes. He'd picked something up from the bedside table and now held it out to her. She gingerly took the photograph, as if she was afraid it might spring to life and bite her.

It showed the two of them next to each other, posing alongside some random staff at the chapel who'd acted as their witnesses.

She read the caption. 'There's a download code for the video…'

'You want to relive the magic?' Alessandro picked up his phone.

Not really—because the flash flood of memories was scalding her with enough humiliation. But it was as if she was stuck on the roller coaster ride from hell.

'We selected the music video option?' she muttered as he scanned the code.

He grinned, apparently as relaxed as ever. 'We're in Vegas—there's every option.'

He scooted a little closer so she could see the screen next to him.

She tried not to blush, but it was impossible.

Set to what she could only describe as a generic boy band ballad—a love song that she didn't recognise but that sounded familiar—a series of appalling images flashed on the screen. She was in her ugly navy skirt and crumpled blouse, while he looked as unbearably handsome as ever, despite that long flight and the horror of the messages they'd got on landing. And he was smiling at her—a smile that made everything inside her light up.

Unable to tear her eyes from the small screen, Katie watched the playback of her exchanging vows and promising to honour him, to *love* him. In the video Alessandro was turning to her with a playful gleam in his eyes. He was framing her face and holding her still...

As if she'd have been able to run when he was looking at her like that. She'd been bolted in place—mesmerised not by his good looks, but by that look in his eyes. That dance of amusement, of warmth and wit underpinned by heat and hunger.

The second he swooped the camera zoomed in. And as a result almost the entire last minute of their wed-

NATALIE ANDERSON   73

ding video showed them kissing. She watched herself ditch the posy of flowers the hotel had provided. She'd dropped it to the floor so she could slide her arms up his body and kiss him back. She'd forgotten anyone else was even present, let alone that there was a camera filming them.

Katie couldn't tear her gaze from the final frozen frame. She'd got married in a cheap nylon skirt. She'd looked just like all those other girls he'd kissed—as hungry, as willing... Except at the same time she didn't. She wasn't glamorous and beautiful and sex kittenish.

And she'd had stars in her eyes.

But he'd had laughter on his face.

Alessandro had pulled back from the kiss first. She'd leaned after him—literally swooning into his embrace. He'd held her upright, away from him. And then he'd laughed. He'd thrown his head back and *laughed*.

It was horrendous.

It wasn't the over-the-top decor of the twenty-four-hour wedding chapel, or even her awful outfit and lack of anything pretty. It was the look on her face. She looked flushed and willing and it was so obvious. She looked *infatuated*. And everyone could see it.

Most of all him.

And now he was almost naked in her bed. But that was only because in her overwrought state at the end of last night she'd *asked* him to stay with her.

When they'd got back to the suite she'd turned to him with tears in her eyes and told him she was tired. He'd come to the bedroom with her and sat down beside her. He'd reassured her. He'd *rescued* her. He'd been a perfect gentleman.

And she must have fallen asleep a second later—like an incompetent, dependent child.

She'd never been as mortified in all her life.

Now he put his phone back on the table with telltale quickness and edged away.

Katie's vulnerable heart thudded as she recognised the horrible truth.

He hadn't wanted to do any of it at all.

Alessandro's head was killing him. Tension, not a hangover. He'd stopped drinking to excess years ago—though admittedly he'd contemplated it earlier as a displacement activity, a distraction to deny the desire coursing through his veins. But he hadn't. Because of Dominque's call.

Hell and damnation.

He'd been so tired last night, so thrown by Katie's visible distress, that he'd seen a quickie marriage as their only option. Memories flitted—her softness and the sweet but tart taste of apricots. He'd kissed her off her feet, and right now he was rocked by the urge to repeat the experience.

Except he'd just seen her appalled expression as the reality of their situation sank in. *Si.* It wasn't his dream deal either.

They'd get it annulled—just as soon as he'd sorted out the estate and care for Susan.

His phone suddenly vibrated. It was still on silent mode after the chapel. He picked it up. It was a message of congratulations. A moment later another message landed. And then more. An influx of congratulations and confusion and appalling curiosity filled his screen.

How?

He gritted his teeth and did a quick online search. Somehow their wedding video had just been uploaded and it was almost immediately trending.

He scooped up the print from the wedding chapel and quickly scanned the information on the back of its cardboard cover.

'It seems I neglected to tick the box refusing my consent for the chapel to use our images for promotional purposes.'

His jaw ached from gritting his teeth so hard. How had he not done a better job of this? He'd been so distracted by her distress and his driving need to somehow make things better. Instead he might have made everything worse.

'Pardon?' Katie's pallor had a greenish tinge to it now.

'The chapel has just posted our wedding video online.'

'What?' She paled even more. 'The video of us…of me…' She trailed off, but he saw her glance down at her crumpled outfit.

Yes, it was hardly the most stunning bridal attire the world had ever seen, and the online trolls were ripping her to shreds already. *Beauty and the Boring* was one comment he *wasn't* about to show her.

Instead he lifted the hotel phone and rapidly ordered coffee and carbs.

'How can you possibly want to eat?' she asked the second he hung up.

'It's exactly what we both need.' Better that hunger than the other one currently tempting him.

His customary headache cure wasn't on the cards today—no lazy sex between soft sheets, no finding relief in the surge of orgasm. Not happening. He'd crossed too many lines with Katie already.

He got out of bed and paced across the room to the window. At the touch of a button the curtains opened. He glared out through the window down to the vibrant avenue below and tried to get his brain to work.

'You were going to back out of it, weren't you?' she said quietly.

He turned and watched certainty settle in her expression.

'You weren't going to go through with it until you found out about the engagement announcement.'

She looked so crushed he had to resist a completely foreign urge to go and give her a cuddle.

'I thought you'd come to your senses once you got far enough away from them,' he admitted. 'That you'd realise getting married wasn't necessary.'

'You brought me all this way to give me time to *come to my senses*?'

'It looked like it was going to take a while,' he conceded.

'But then Brian sprang that announcement on us.'

Alessandro hadn't been able to come up with a decent alternative at the time. He'd been compelled into action by the fear in her eyes. They hadn't even arranged a prenuptial agreement, or discussed the amount he was going to pump into the property, or how he'd recover that cost. Or anything.

She drew up her knees, covering herself with the sheet. 'You think I'm pathetic, don't you?'

'I think you're...' He paused and tried to think how best to explain the confusing things he thought and felt about her. 'You're sweet. Perhaps a little...naive.'

She winced. 'But you can't say you're going to do something and then go back on your word.' Her temper flared. 'That's not fair. Especially something as important as this.'

'But I did it.' He gestured to the unfortunate photo on the table. 'Now you've got a husband to protect you.'

She stared at him.

'Well, wife?' He eyed her grimly, barely holding back the anger that surged within him. 'What's next on the list?'

She shook her head slowly. 'We can get it annulled, right? You didn't really want this. We should just... figure out another way. I'm so sorry.'

He was taken aback by her unexpected stand—and the dignity in her apology.

'Maybe that would make an even bigger scandal?' she wondered aloud, looking almost hopeful. 'I've run away to Vegas on a whim...created a crazy twenty-four-hour wedding scandal... Brian will hate it.'

Something contrary swirled in his gut. Truth be told, he no longer cared about what her foster father thought or wanted. He was suddenly angry with her for wanting to walk away already, when he'd moved heaven and earth to do what she'd wanted.

He didn't want to rush into another set of actions that would make things even worse. Because it was impacting on him *now*.

'I might have a certain reputation,' he said coolly. 'But that's a step too far even for me. We're not getting an annulment. We'll stick with your original plan. Six months, minimum. Even that's a little on the short side.'

'But you didn't even want six days...' she argued, appalled. 'Five was enough for you, wasn't it? You didn't even mean to use those—you were just stringing me along, patting me on the head and saying *sure thing, sweetie*—pacifying me like a child.'

She was angry? Well, so was he.

'I don't *pacify* anyone. I just say no. And I'm saying no to the annulment idea. You made this bed, *dolcezza*, you might as well get comfortable.'

Her eyes widened and her focus skimmed over his body again. Every muscle within him tensed. He shouldn't be thinking about being back in bed with her. Last night she'd been vulnerable and scared…and so soft. He'd not wanted to leave her alone and distressed. He'd fallen asleep still clothed, waking only enough to shuck his shirt and trousers off before curling around her warm body again.

Now Alessandro stalked back to the bed and scooped up his phone. He needed to get on top of this. And to do that they needed to get away from the scene of their madness before any paparazzi turned up. He was no celebrity, but he had money, and celebrities used some of his properties.

'We need the plane,' he said as soon as Dominique answered. 'Departing in two hours.'

'Anything else I can arrange?' Dominique asked.

Alessandro winced at the almost breathless curiosity Dominique was hiding. She'd clearly heard the news too. 'I'll message you with the destination and other details shortly.'

'We're leaving already?' Katie frowned as he ended the call.

He felt a perverse need to provoke her. 'Yes. We're going on our honeymoon.'

'Honeymoon?' Colour flooded not just her face but her neck, and all the skin he could see…

Her wide-eyed gaze dipped to his bare chest again. He could almost feel it, like a caress on his skin, and he suddenly ached for the reality of her touch.

'It'll give us time and space to sort out the next six months,' he snapped, bending to pick up his trousers and turning his back on her.

Going into any takeover, he needed all the 'i's dotted and the 't's crossed. He'd get his team to work out all the options regarding the marriage, then he'd get Susan's care sorted, acquire Brian's debt and stockpile the ammunition to ensure his compliance. He started mentally drafting emails—anything to stop himself from thinking about getting back into bed and taking up the offer in her beautiful eyes.

'But I need to get back to Susan—'

'You asked for my help, Katie. Let me get on with it.'

'But—'

'Trust me to do my thing,' he interrupted again roughly. 'I'll explain later.'

There was only one place to go. 'Okay.'

At the chastened obedience in her voice he swung back to look at her. She was watching him warily, and then she looked down. He hated it that she'd gone quiet on him.

'I need a shower…' She trailed off. Tension surged in the atmosphere.

She also needed clothes.

He struggled to breathe. 'I'll get some stuff sent up while you're in there,' he offered huskily.

She shot him an embarrassed look as she awkwardly

got out of bed and smoothed down her crumpled skirt. 'Thanks.'

He couldn't help grabbing her arm as she passed him. The colour in her cheeks deepened as she looked up into his eyes. He needed to get to know her better—slice through this tension enough to get them to a point where they could coexist happily for a while.

But how did they stop the chemical reaction between them igniting?

Inner tension tightened his grip. 'Just so you know, I'm not agreeing to extra-marital affairs. For either of us.'

He felt her tiny shiver, but she held his gaze with that determined one of her own.

'Fine. But just so *you* know, I'm not agreeing to anything intimate. This is a marriage on paper only.'

Really?

He smiled. The electricity flowing through his veins chased away his headache.

Alessandro was all for making the most of his opportunities—and his acquisitions. And he was going to have so much fun teasing her. Because there was no way she could deny their chemistry any more than he could.

'Fine.' He echoed her with soft sarcasm. 'Of course you're welcome to change your mind any time. I won't hold it against you if you do.'

Because he'd held her in his arms already, and he'd kissed her, heard her moans. And, if he so wanted, he'd have her mind changed in minutes.

CHAPTER FIVE

KATIE HAD DISCOVERED an appalling appreciation of Alessandro's obscene wealth. Being whisked through airport security with privacy and speed like some VIP had been jaw-dropping, and there was a lot to be said for the luxury of a private jet. As the plane now levelled out after take-off she sank deeper into the plush leather seat. The speed of it all was good. The sooner they got back to White Oaks the better.

'Go and lie down in comfort.' Alessandro tore his attention away from his tablet to send her a searching look. 'You're barely able to keep your eyes open. We'll be in the air for a few hours yet—plenty of time for you to get a decent rest.'

She couldn't. It was only now that she had a moment to think that she realised she'd forgotten the most important thing.

'I should have phoned Susan,' she muttered. 'She'll be so worried. I never go this long without contact.'

She was shocked at how selfish she'd been. Alessandro had moved so quickly she'd simply been swept along on the tide of his dynamism. But that wasn't good enough.

'There's already been contact,' he replied easily.

'Pardon?' She stared at him.

'My team,' he explained. 'The lawyers have already made contact with Brian while you were in the shower.'

'Your first contact was through *lawyers*?' In a split second her nerves had tensed to total strain.

'It's fine.' He smiled, but his expression seemed more wicked than reassuring. 'They've made Brian an offer he can't refuse. Don't worry. White Oaks is safe.'

Don't worry? Her heart pounded. 'What about Susan?'

'We're engaging nurse companions. She'll have round-the-clock assistance. Something she should have had for months already.'

At that simply spoken truth the sickening heat of shame swept over her. She'd always tried her best for her foster mother, but now her inadequate efforts made her shrink.

'Brian's accepted that?' He'd never liked people in the house. Had always insisted she and Susan could cope on their own.

'He either accepts my terms or we make him bankrupt. But even if he chooses that option White Oaks and Susan will be cared for.'

Katie blinked rapidly. 'Just like that?'

'Brian's not stupid. He'll agree.' Alessandro said with arrogant certainty. 'Especially if he *loves* her.'

His bitter edge made her look at him. Was he so cynical he didn't believe in love? Why? She blinked again. Would he ever love anyone enough to sacrifice everything for them?

Inwardly she rejected the idea. He was so self-sufficient and self-assured he'd never *need* to sacrifice everything. He'd simply figure out a bunch of alternative solutions. He was too capable. And she felt too useless.

She watched as he went back to his work, typing on the tablet's keyboard like a demon. Astute and agile in his dealings, he was a fast mover—snapping up acquisitions with speed before other buyers even spotted the opportunity. Now he was ferociously dealing with the disaster she'd created, and his ruthless, uncompromising streak was exposed as he coolly exerted his authority over Brian.

His kind of confidence was something she doubted she'd ever have. All her life she'd been insecure— always worrying that she'd displease Brian to the point where he'd refuse to house her any more. She'd tried hard to curb her inclination to fight back, working instead to pacify him—staying out of sight, not raising her voice, not being an inconvenience or an embarrassment.

She'd done that for herself, but also because the emotional strain on Susan had been almost as bad. When Brian was in a good mood he was generous and gregarious, showering her foster mother with love and affection... And in those occasional moments Katie had finally felt safe. But those moments had been short, and always broken by periods of glowering moods, snapped commands and veiled threats.

She was to remember her place—where she'd come from—and she should always be *grateful*.

Now she'd irrevocably altered their relationship by brutally defying his crazy 'marry Carl Westin' request. She was finally away from Brian's control.

But Alessandro was doing everything. She'd gone from one powerful man to another...and that truth sat uncomfortably within her.

Making it worse was her infatuation. There was no other word for the way she'd looked at Alessandro at their wedding—in a way that everyone who saw that video would see…

There was only one thing she could do. She needed to step up, take the responsibility onto her own shoulders somehow. For now that meant falling back on her old survival skills—staying out of sight, staying quiet—while she built her strength and came up with her own plan.

So she did as he'd suggested and retreated to the safety of the sleeping quarters, where she couldn't stare at him like some starstruck teen with a crush.

On the bed, she pulled up one of the soft blankets to cover her legs. The comfy jeans and cute Las Vegas tee that he'd magicked up for her from that hotel's gift shop were great, but she was cold.

As she lay down her mind whirled through replays of the previous night—Alessandro's decisiveness and speed. Her own relief. And then those moments when she'd woken this morning, to find him in bed with her, so full of his amusement at her embarrassment…

She listened to the rhythm of his fingers stabbing at the keyboard over the hum of the plane's engine. And in that dusky dream space between waking and sleeping she let herself remember the warm comfort of his embrace and finally relaxed…

'Katie?'

She felt the mattress suddenly depress and swiftly sat up.

'I managed to spend a whole night in your bed without ravishing you.' Sardonic amusement flashed in his eyes as he shifted to sit more comfortably on the side of the bed. 'You don't need to be afraid of me.'

'I'm not afraid of you,' she argued instantly.

'You're afraid of yourself, then.' That gleam in his gaze intensified.

She rolled her eyes, despite her suddenly sprinting heart. 'Are you ever serious?'

'All the time.'

Something within her tingled—caution. For all his playboy flirtation she felt he was telling the truth. That compelled her to deflect the conversation away from the personal. 'How long have we been flying?'

'We've less than an hour to go.'

'Oh, good.' She'd slept through most of the flight.

'You think?'

An edgy expression tightened his features. She shifted an inch further away. He noticed, huffing out a breath before he rubbed at his forehead.

'There really wasn't any other guy you wanted to run away with?' he suddenly asked softly. 'You didn't have some boyfriend back in the village who Brian tried to chase off?'

Her mouth dried at the intrusiveness of the question. Wordlessly, slowly, she shook her head.

'What about those students who picked the fruit at the end of summer? There were always lots of those.' He waited, a frown growing in his gaze. 'You didn't flirt with any of them over the years?'

She knew *he'd* enjoyed those students—but she hadn't. She'd been far too shy, and far too aware of risking the wrath of her foster father or disappointing her too-gentle foster mother. Besides, none of them had ever so much as looked at her.

The one time she'd put on some lipstick a school friend had given her, Brian had seen it.

'You look cheap.'

His belittling comment hadn't just been unkind, he'd laughed as he'd said it. In one breath he'd killed Katie's desire to try and attract someone. So she'd repressed her youthful yearning for attention, refused to acknowledge her own secret needs. Because he'd confirmed what she'd known already—she couldn't get it right. She wasn't enough as she was. She'd probably never be enough.

Alessandro was still watching her closely, more serious than she'd ever seen him. 'You've had no boyfriends at all, Katie?'

She shook her head yet again.

'Not ever?' His voice tightened. 'So you've not—?'

'No.' She forestalled any further highly embarrassing questions angrily. 'No boyfriends. No kissing. No sex. No *nothing*.'

He sat very still, his gaze not leaving hers. 'I don't think I've ever met a woman in her twenties who's still a virgin. It's not that common, Katie.'

He said it as if there was something wrong with her. Of course it had to be *her*—yet again *she* was the one at fault.

'Maybe not in the circles *you* hang out in, but I don't think it's that abnormal,' she said stiffly, barely masking her inner rebellion. 'No doubt I'm the most untouched woman you've ever met. And you've *married* me. The irony is extreme, don't you think?'

She tossed her head—embarrassed, defensive and wary...but mostly with herself. With that little weakness she had within her when it came to him.

'Does Carl know you've not had a boyfriend?

She paused, horrified at the question. 'I don't know.' She stared down at the blanket covering her. 'You think he wanted to marry me because of that? Like I was some kind of virgin sacrifice?' She rejected the idea completely. 'Marriage is for a long time. Brian could've just offered him the use of my body for a night…'

Suddenly she was bitterly hurt. Anger forced her to look back into Alessandro's too-handsome face.

'You can't think why he'd want me for a wife at all, can you?'

'I can't understand why *anyone* would want a wife at all,' he countered calmly. 'Or a husband, for that matter. It's not you personally.'

'And yet here you are, married to me,' she pointed out.

Alessandro stared back at her. They were locked in a still, silent moment.

'I think Carl wanted someone controllable. A doormat,' she finally said, slicing through the strained atmosphere.

'You're not *that* controllable,' he muttered.

'No. I'm not.' She lifted her chin, embracing the defiance he sparked within her. 'And I'm not going to struggle with six months' celibacy because I've been uninterested in *that* all my life,' she said scornfully.

Desperately she wanted to believe her own words. Desperately she wanted to score a point against him because he made her so uncomfortable.

But he didn't rise to her bait, he only goaded her more—with that smile.

'I don't think you're "uninterested" in that,' he said softly.

'You can't imagine *anyone* being uninterested,' Katie scoffed.

'Lame call, Katie.' He sent her another considering look from beneath those long, dark lashes. 'You might be inexperienced, but you're not that immature.' He paused, his head cocked. 'Who gave you your first kiss?'

She stared down at the blanket between them and refused to answer.

'Katie…?'

The hint of appalled incredulity in his voice let her know he'd figured it out.

'Don't let it go to your head,' she gritted.

'It's not going to my *head*,' he drawled wickedly.

'Really?' She lifted her chin and glared at him. 'Do guys seriously get off on this?'

He laughed, but it didn't sound easy. 'Don't try to distract me. Denial is unworthy of you, *dolcezza*. I've kissed you. You kissed me back.'

'And let's agree not to do it again.'

He shook his head. 'You are afraid—why?' He frowned at her as if she was a conundrum. 'If you've waited this long there *has* to be a reason.'

Oh, he had to be kidding…

But his insistent prying had pushed her past her learned reticence. She'd make him as uncomfortable as he made her.

'Maybe I was waiting to give my virginity to my husband,' she said in dulcet tones, and sent him a demure look. 'That's a reason why a lot of women wait.'

He stared at her, as still as a predator waiting for his moment to pounce, an unreadable expression on his face.

She rolled her eyes again, masking the intensity this conversation was building within her. 'The only reasons I'm a virgin are lack of interest and lack of opportunity.'

That devilish look lit within him. 'Why, how convenient... You have both now...' he murmured.

Surely he didn't mean—?

He leaned closer. '*I'm* interested. *I'm* your opportunity.'

She just stared at him.

'Right here, right now. We both know how well we'd get on together. What do you say, Katie?'

She was almost certain he wasn't serious, but the awful thing was part of her had already melted in complete surrender...and she was angry with both herself *and* him for that.

'I say I'm not interested.'

His smile swerved. 'Are you sure about that?'

Her breathing quickened. 'I also say you're mean.'

'Opportunity is *not* the only reason.' His lips twisted in mockery as he proved her a liar. 'Are you waiting for love, Katie?'

'Well... I'd have to at least *like* the guy,' she retorted furiously, pushed to the extreme.

He winced and pressed his hand to his heart. 'After all I've done for you...?'

'Don't tease.' She borrowed his look from under lowered eyelashes. 'I'm no match for you.'

He stared for a second, then laughed. 'And that little pretence shows just how up to my weight you are, Katie. You're quiet because you've had to be—not because you didn't have something to say. You're not entirely shy.'

He reached out and grabbed her hand, flattening her fingers when she tried to curl them into a fist.

'You're going to have to get used to a little touching, Katie.' He traced circles on her palm with his index finger as he spoke. 'If you want to prevent Susan from being anxious you'll have to present a blissfully happy façade to her. You said it yourself: you'll have to fake it. You'll need to look and act like you're in love with me and you can't talk to her until you're certain you can do that.'

He spoke lightly, but she understood that he meant every word.

'I'm not having the world know this marriage is a sham. You wanted this, you've got it, but you'll have to act the part. I will touch you. I will kiss you. Everyone knows I'd never be cold with my wife.'

She realised that beneath that tease, even as he touched her so softly, he was angry.

'I've seduced you away from your fiancé after all,' he mocked. 'You're going to have to look spellbound.'

Waves of heat rose just from those tiny tickling circles. His skilful fingers cast sensations like confetti—skating caresses that sent shivers of anticipation down her spine.

She swallowed the hard lump in her throat. 'You're sure that isn't for your own ego?'

'You know my ego doesn't need the boost.' He held her hand more tightly and leaned closer. 'You can't blush every time I come within two feet of you. You can't pull away or look shy...'

She didn't want to pull away. Unfortunately she suspected he knew that too.

'We're going to need to practise,' he added softly.

'You're kidding?'

He shook his head and smiled wickedly. 'As serious as ever—that's me.'

With that he tugged her closer and pressed his mouth on hers. It was a teasing, light kiss, one she could have broken from easily. But she didn't. Instead she stilled, uncertain whether to push him away or kiss him back. Then her body overruled her brain and decided for her and she leaned closer.

Instantly he slid his other hand to the nape of her neck, holding her so he could kiss her even more deeply. His lips roved gently, firmly, and his tongue stroked in a light tease. His fingers still clasped hers. His touch felt beyond intimate, bathing her in rose-gold heat. He was warm and strong and giving.

Delightful, dizzying wisps of wonder trickled through her veins. She tasted his smile in his kiss and somehow she smiled too. Who'd have thought kissing could be so easy or feel so right?

Yet the second she thought that a flicker of something else rose. Once again he'd unleashed something long hidden—something so sharp she wasn't quite ready for it. But she couldn't stop. She couldn't pull back. The desire to keep kissing, keep touching, keep connected to him was too strong.

This was a mistake. Alessandro wrestled with his conscience and his want, but his ability to reason was slipping further the longer he had his mouth sealed to hers. The longer he lost himself in her sweetness. And she was so very sweet.

Anyway, since when did he even have a conscience? There was nothing wrong with just kissing. It was simple fun that meant little…only short moments to enjoy.

But she was a virgin. And she was also his wife.

Those facts clawed at his gut. How was he supposed to stop their chemistry from combusting for six whole months? It was an impossible ask.

He forced himself to break the kiss, lifting his head to stare down at her. Her heavy-lidded eyes contained a dazed sparkle and her lips looked soft and lush and reddened. Her ragged breathing gave her away, as did the building heat of her skin beneath his fingertips.

She was no porcelain doll, no unfeeling automaton. She was full-bodied and hot and the sexiest thing he'd seen... And he'd never wanted a woman the way he wanted her now.

With a muffled groan he slammed his mouth back on hers, pulling her fully into his arms, needing to feel her against his chest. She was as soft and lithe as he'd imagined. And he was doing them both a favour, *si*? Their marriage would look real enough and they'd rid themselves of the frustration riding them both. She'd become a little more worldly...

His reasons, justifications, excuses faded as he succumbed to the pleasure of caressing her. He obeyed the driving urge to touch more, taste more. He pushed gently so she fell back onto the bed and he followed, his body tensing as he felt her hands slide to his waist.

He kissed her neck, marvelling at her soft, smooth skin. He ached to touch every inch of her. He swept his hand down to her hip, feeling the supple arch of her body, listening to the rise of her breathing and then another of those little moans, followed by a gasp as she tried to catch it back. Hell, he loved those moans of hers.

He toyed with the hem of her tee, tempted to lift it and seek out the even softer skin of her waist, her breasts. He'd kiss and caress them until the pleasure sent them both insane...

'Stop...' she said in a small breathless voice. 'Alessandro, please stop.'

He froze, cold shock tossing immediate regret over him. He'd lost control when he never did. But he'd thought she was with him.

He braced his fists either side of her and pushed up, refusing to give in to the overriding urge to touch her again. Her eyes were closed, and her full mouth was turned down in an expression of complete misery. Had he misread all those signs he thought he'd felt?

'Katie...?' he questioned hoarsely.

'You don't have to...' She trailed off.

Confused, he watched the emotions flicker across her face as he tried to get his brain to catch up with her conversation. He didn't 'have to' what?

'You've proved your point, okay? I'm...' She drew in a shuddering breath. 'You don't have to do anything more.'

Wait—so this wasn't about her not wanting more... this was about her thinking that *he* didn't want more?

He was utterly thrown. The low burn of shame angered him—because her accusation was partly true. Hadn't he wanted her surrender? Hadn't he plotted to tease her, to prove she wanted him? But that had been for ever ago. Within two seconds of touching her all pretence, all game-playing, had burned away, revealing the raw reality of the attraction between them.

'This isn't about me *proving* anything, Katie,' he said bluntly.

She still didn't look at him. 'Like I said, I'm no match for you,' she muttered.

'I kissed you because I wanted to. I want *you*. Because, as infuriating as you are, you're also fascinating and I want to touch you. Everywhere. Sorry if you find that offensive.'

Rosy colour swarmed over her skin and she finally opened her captivating eyes. 'You think I'm fascinating?'

'And infuriating,' he repeated bluntly. But he couldn't help smiling at her.

Her glare was impressive, but undermined by the fact that she was still frozen with shy awkwardness on the bed before him.

'I thought you were just… I thought it was just a game.'

'Katie.' He half laughed, half sighed. 'It's *always* a game. That's what sex *is*. I enjoy baiting you, but only because I genuinely want you.'

He leaned closer. Provoking her was more fun than he'd had in ages. But touching her was shockingly sublime. And quite possibly addictive.

Her baleful expression didn't ease. 'Because I'm inexperienced?'

'Are you really this insecure?' he growled. 'I've kissed you every chance I got, in case you hadn't noticed. Long before I knew that you were inexperienced. If anything, that puts me off.' He rolled his eyes. 'We shouldn't… *I* shouldn't.'

'I'm sorry if it's an inconvenience,' she said sarcastically. 'Maybe it's hard for me to believe when no one's ever wanted me before.'

He laughed. But then swiftly sobered as he realised that in that last she had been entirely serious. A powerful harsh heat built inside him—something more than desire.

'That's only because you've been hiding.'

He glanced down at the jeans and tee she wore. They revealed only a hint of her figure. She had cute curves, and long legs for a short person. She should be more confident—the way she was when she talked about her work.

Tension swelled within him again. 'I'm not sure we can keep this a marriage on paper only, Katie.'

The likelihood of them getting to six months without having sex was virtually nil. The chemistry he felt, she felt too.

She'd been sheltered—imprisoned, actually—but he would show her the world if she'd let him. Both literally and in this most personal of spheres. She was warm and sweet, passionate and strong. And they'd be free to continue with their lives at the conclusion...

He suddenly stood, turning away as he grappled with the discomforting thought of her being free to find someone else after their marriage had ended. The thought of some other man making her moan in that soft, pleading way she had when he'd kissed her. It had been a primal purr, asking for more. But the thought of some other man being the first to show her just what she'd been created to do...

He clenched his jaw. With one damn kiss everything had changed. This was everything he didn't want. He was ill-cast in this role of rescuer. He'd never wanted marriage. He wasn't cut out to make that 'for ever' commitment to one person. But they were locked in it now, and he was going to have to exert better self-control.

Katie constantly blushed because she was an inexperienced romantic. He couldn't be further from either of those things.

And now her silence spoke volumes.

Too late he remembered her offer to pay him back any time, anyhow. Did she think this was the *how*? Revulsion and regret at the power imbalance between them surged. She'd been raised to be too polite—required not just to be obedient, but *subservient*.

Did she feel as if she couldn't say no to him now he'd married her? The thought of her saying yes only to please him, or because she felt she owed him, was horrific. But she'd responded to him—he knew she had—and he'd stopped the second she'd asked him to. He could and would always do that.

'I want you,' he said roughly, unused to admitting anything he felt deeply. And this was beyond deep. 'But I'll only do what you want me to. And you have to *really* want it Katie.'

She had to want it the way he did.

Almost uncontrollably.

Desperately he glanced at his watch and made himself walk further away. 'We've less than thirty minutes till we land.'

'Will we go straight to see Susan?'

He froze, then turned back to face her. 'We're not landing in England, Katie.'

'What?' Her eyes rounded. 'Where are we going?'

'Italy.'

And the sooner they got there, the sooner he could straighten out his head and regain control over his wayward body.

But he couldn't resist one last tease. 'We're going on our honeymoon, remember?'

CHAPTER SIX

KATIE WAS SWEPT along on the tide of Alessandro's dynamism all over again. She'd never encountered someone who could get so much done in so little time or with such apparent ease. They'd landed, cleared Customs, been ensconced in another gorgeous car and driven to another fabulous hotel.

Completely different from Las Vegas, this was a beachside hotel, next to a harbour filled with billionaires' yachts and stylish people drinking coffee and looking impossibly glamorous even at this early hour of the morning.

Feeling hot and sticky and tired, Katie wanted to skulk into a corner and hide.

Alessandro was pure practicality again, turning to her the second they were alone in another large suite. 'You need more clothes. Do you want help selecting them?'

She did need more clothes, but there had to be a limit to what she could take from him—besides which, she really felt like arguing with him.

'I am not parading a selection of outfits in front of you like some...some *courtesan*,' she said stiffly.

He smiled appreciatively. 'I didn't mean me. I don't

have the time to take you shopping,' he derided softly. 'Anyway, I'd rather see you getting out of clothes than into them. I meant would you like a personal shopper? Like a stylist?'

He thought she needed one. Katie sank into another mire of embarrassment, furiously trying to think of some smart retort and failing. Because the fact was she'd had very few sartorial options until now. The local village didn't have any particularly stylish stores, and since Brian's stinging judgement that one time she'd dressed up she'd hidden in baggy jeans and tees.

But she wanted to take charge of herself, didn't she? Perhaps she could surprise Alessandro? Because, judging by that gleam of amusement in his eyes, he thought she'd be annoyed by his offer.

On one level she was, but on another she was quite grateful. Truthfully, she had no idea what to wear, and for once in her life she wanted to look good.

'Actually, yes, please. I think a makeover might be just the thing to lift my confidence.' A spark of defiance lit within her. She wanted to look *better* than good. 'Maybe I can look like people would expect your wife to—should I get short skirts? Low-cut tops? Totter about in heels?'

'Are you judging other women by their clothing choices?' he queried blandly.

She took the hit—she deserved it. Hadn't she just done to nameless, faceless other women what Brian had done to her? She deserved better from herself. And she needed to allow herself to deserve better too.

'Point taken.' She licked her lips awkwardly. 'So... thank you. I appreciate the offer and I'd like the help.'

Something kindled in his eyes, but he seemed to smother his smile. 'I'll arrange it.'

Being Alessandro, he made the call immediately, speaking rapidly in Italian.

'She's on her way,' he informed her after a few minutes. 'Don't worry about the budget. You'll need casual, and perhaps a couple of outfits suitable for evening functions. I'm going to work for a few hours—I'll be here when you get back.'

Katie stared at him, struck again by his ability to make things happen. 'Do you work all the time?'

He shot her an amused look. 'You know the answer to that.'

'Work hard, play hard?' She shook her head. 'Such a cliché, Alessandro.'

'Are you sure you want to keep baiting me, Katie?'

She was saved from that lethal whisper by a knock on the door.

Alessandro swiftly crossed the room. Katie was struck with sudden nerves as a slim brunette walked in. Dressed in black, with beautiful make-up and her hair in a sleek chignon, she strode confidently straight up to Katie with an appraising gaze.

'I am Julia,' the woman declared, as if Katie ought to be impressed. 'This will be good, *si*?' She studied Katie again and nodded, as if pleased. 'You have great structure.'

Nonplussed, Katie couldn't think what to reply.

Alessandro murmured something in Italian to Julia, which left Katie feeling gauche and clueless and as if she was being dismissed. But it was Alessandro who stood to leave.

He paused beside her on his way and whispered

in her ear. 'Don't dress to please me, her, your foster parents or anyone else. Dress to please yourself.' He brushed his lips against her cheekbone, the light touch leaving a burn on her skin. 'I dare you.'

Katie's pulse skidded. She had *carte blanche* with a credit card, complete self-expression and she had no idea what to do.

But it turned out that with Julia—stylist to Italian stars—personal shopping didn't mean traipsing around a bunch of shops and getting exhausted. Personal shopping with Julia meant Katie being ensconced in the hotel beauty salon to spend an hour perusing various lookbooks online and discussing the styles that appealed to her.

Julia made notes and sent messages on her phone. Then she led Katie to a team of beauticians to be buffed and polished to gleaming perfection. She enjoyed both salt and sugar scrubs and rubs, a manicure, pedicure, a haircut, a facial and a make-up lesson. Meanwhile Julia sourced a huge variety of garments.

'We'll create the perfect capsule wardrobe for your honeymoon,' Julia announced with her thick Italian accent. 'A combination of casual, dressy, totally sexy. He says to please yourself, and that is good, but you can also make *him* speechless, *si*?'

He'd told Julia that Katie had to please herself? Shaking her head, Katie tried on literally dozens of dresses, skirts, trousers, blouses, tees… And slowly she got into it. It was impossible not to discover the joy of soft, fine fabrics—silk, cashmere, linen. She wasn't used to wearing clothing that was so beautifully tailored.

'This flatters your subtle femininity.' Julia nodded

in approval as Katie emerged from the dressing room in a floral dress with a deep neckline.

'Subtle' was right. Katie ruefully studied her reflection. Making the most of her meagre assets still didn't turn her into anything like those models Alessandro was so often photographed with.

Pull yourself together. None of this pity.

She was his wife for a few weeks—she couldn't complain. And she did look better than she'd ever looked. She was *passable*.

'Try this as well.' Julia smiled at her as if she'd found missing treasure.

Katie stared at the tiny metallic bikini Julia held out to her. 'I'm not sure…'

'It will highlight your eyes. He'll be…how do you say?…putty in your hands.'

While that was a tempting thought, the truth was more the other way around.

Julia grabbed her phone. 'I am going to lay the clothes out in a variety of looks, so you have some ideas to scroll through and select.'

'Thank you.' Katie decided that Julia was worth her weight in gold.

'You're leaving this evening, so I'll pack the things you do not need today and the porters will bring the bags up to your room.'

Katie simply nodded, hiding the embarrassing fact that she had no idea of Alessandro's plans while this paid stylist apparently did.

An hour later she finally returned to their suite. Alessandro had his back to her and was talking in rapid Italian, seemingly endlessly, on the phone. With his shirtsleeves rolled up, and surrounded by pieces of paper, two tablets and a laptop, he looked every inch the busy entrepreneur.

He didn't turn as she walked in, which was fabulous—because she didn't want to endure his appraisal and sardonic compliments on her haircut and new clothes. That would just be awkward.

So she chose not to wait or to interrupt him. She'd check out the pool instead. She was uncomfortably hot all of a sudden.

In the luxurious changing room, she slipped into the bikini and scooped up the shawl Julia had told her to accessorise it with, and slid on the matching bronze sandals.

It wasn't until she was sitting on the edge of the pool, paddling her feet, that she had a qualm of guilt over just how much Julia had encouraged her to buy.

She'd somehow lost her head in that deliciously scented room, with all those beautiful flowers and gleaming mirrors, and Julia had made her feel as if it was perfectly normal to buy six pairs of shoes, seven dresses and a huge assortment of skirts, trousers and tops. Not to mention the beauty case Julia had also insisted she needed—and the curling wand for her hair, the make-up, the moisturiser and the special sunscreen... And then there were the leather luggage bags to put all the clothes in...

Far too late Katie realised she'd bought far too much. She paddled her feet faster. She was going to have to apologise to Alessandro and then beg Julia to take half the stuff back. It could be returned, right?

Pondering how best to extricate herself from this latest mess, she laughed beneath her breath at her own

uselessness. So much for letting herself deserve more...
accept more.

'Katie?'

She turned at the husky calling of her name, still
smiling at her own madness.

'Alessandro...' She bit her lip, unsure how to con-
fess. 'You've finished your work?'

He towered over her, his hands on his hips as he surveyed her. She couldn't see his expression behind the
sunglasses he'd put on. But when he didn't say anything
more she had the sense he was irritated in some way.

*It's not necessarily anything to do with you...it could
be work.*

'You were busy. I didn't want to bother you.'

He glanced about the pool, his eyebrows drawing
together as he looked at the other guests.

'I wanted to cool off,' she added when he still didn't
answer.

'Here.' He picked up the beautiful wrap Julia had
included and handed it to her. 'Put this on.'

She clutched it close, shocked mortification chilling
her. Was the bikini awful? Was he embarrassed by her?

He suddenly hunched down beside her and pulled off
his sunglasses so he could glare into her eyes. 'Don't
look so terrified.' He reached out and ran his forefinger
along her bare shoulder. 'Your skin is too fair to sit so
exposed in the sun. Either I rub sunscreen on you or
you cover up. It's your choice.'

He was concerned about her *skin* burning? Suddenly
she was all but incinerating on the spot from the brilliant fire in his blue eyes.

'I've already put lotion on,' she whispered.

She didn't want his hands on her body again. At least not in public. She wasn't sure she'd cope.

'There are people watching us,' he whispered back, a reluctant smile tugging his mouth into that tempting curve. 'You might want to rethink your scowl.'

There were? She pulled the wrap over her shoulders and made herself smile.

'Good choice,' he drawled. 'We're leaving in twenty minutes. I understand your bags are ready?'

'Why are we leaving? This place is amazing.'

'Amazing is acceptable, but I prefer paradise.'

She relaxed at the return of his arrogance. 'Big promises.' She arched her eyebrows at him. 'Is paradise another plane ride away?'

'Are you finding that relentless round-the-world travel isn't everything?' He chuckled. 'Don't worry, it's just a short hop by helicopter.' He glanced down at the almost sheer wrap she'd covered herself with. 'You can stay in the bikini if you want. I don't mind.'

She wasn't staying in the bikini.

'Did you have fun today?' he asked slyly as he accompanied her back to their suite.

'Actually, I think I spent too much,' she confessed in a breathless guilty rush. 'Far too much. I think I got a bit excited by it all and just said yes to everything.'

He laughed. 'Excellent. That is good practice.'

'I'm sorry…'

'Of course you are sorry, *dolcezza*,' he murmured. 'And here I was, thinking you were making progress.'

She frowned, unsure what he meant. 'I'll pay you back.'

'I'm sure you will think of a way.' He chuckled again, as her blush burned like a fever, and lifted a finger to feel the heat flaming her cheeks for himself. 'Your mind, Katie… I'm beginning to think it's *filthy*.'

'No, it's the way you say everything that makes it all seem so…*naughty*,' she grumbled awkwardly. 'You're a tease.'

'Yes.' He nodded. 'I suppose I am. But it's just words. My payment is the pleasure I get from seeing you like this.' He gazed into her eyes. 'Confident and smiling,' he explained softly. 'Nothing more. You don't have to please me. You have only to please yourself.'

He expected nothing more from her?

Katie fought off an absurd feeling of disappointment. He might want her, but he didn't have the desperate desire she did. Somehow she needed to rein in her own pulse.

CHAPTER SEVEN

As the helicopter rose up from the roof of the hotel Katie's death grip on her safety belt slackened, as did her jaw, because the view was so stunning she forgot her first-time flier nerves. Speechless, she stared at the sparkling water, studded with sleek, gleaming boats. It was a vast crystalline playground for the ultra-stylish, famous and fabulous, and it went on for as far as she could see.

For almost twenty minutes they flew high and fast, and she gazed in wonder at the emerald coast and the scattered array of small islands. Then they began descending, right above one. High cliffs rose on one side, while stone walls bracketed a small beach on the other. In the middle a breathtaking building stood amongst verdant perfectly planted gardens. Hewn from traditional stone, accented with tiles and glass, it was a modern architectural masterpiece, designed to enhance and appreciate the majestic vista.

Katie's heart skidded at the beauty of it. And at the isolation.

She caught a glimpse of a couple of smaller structures in the distance before they landed on the helipad. Then Katie's stomach fluttered as she ducked and ran alongside Alessandro, conscious of his firm arm across her shoulders. Only moments later the helicopter lifted up again.

'Please don't tell me you own this island,' she breathed, conscious of the sudden silence.

'What should I say instead?' His smile chased the remnants of a frown from his face and he drew in a deep breath.

But Katie's lungs had tightened. 'You have staff?' she asked, trying to sound casual.

'A couple who usually live onsite act as caretakers.' He scooped up the bags the co-pilot had left for them. 'They've gone to the mainland for a few days.'

Leaving her utterly alone with him?

Her nerves flipped from that light flutter to a loud jangle.

Ironic speculation turned his eyes an even more brilliant blue. 'Shall I show you around?'

Katie followed him along the path towards the house. The gardens were gorgeous—established trees offered shade and privacy, while flowers filled the air with a sweet, summery scent.

'It's big for just you,' she murmured, trying to distract herself from her too-intense thoughts.

'I sometimes lease it out when I'm not here,' he answered lightly. 'It's an investment as much as anything.'

Yes, people would pay huge amounts to spend time in such a private, perfect escape. It was architecturally impressive and luxurious, offering a rare level of comfort with space enough for a party.

A shard of cold reality pierced the sweet air. She'd bet he'd had some hedonistic, decadent parties here.

She could just imagine millions of beautiful women in their bikinis, draped around the pool.

Alessandro didn't take her to the towering main entrance, but led her to a vast, plant-lined terrace, with a beautiful blue swimming pool that ran down the side of the building. He walked half the length of the terrace, then opened the fourth set of double doors and stood back to let her enter.

'This is your bedroom.'

She felt a quicksilver urge to flee, but instead she stepped through. The room was airy, light and luxurious, with soft-looking furnishings and a huge bed. Transfixed, she licked her dry lips, trying to stop the immediate surge of rampantly inappropriate thoughts in her head.

'It's beautiful, thank you.'

Too awkward to move, she watched him set her bags at the end of the bed. 'I'm down the hall,' he said. 'Near if you need me.'

She shot him a quick look and glanced back to her bags, half wishing she could snatch them up and escape. Yet at the same time the last thing she wanted to do was run from him.

'You didn't want to be alone last night,' Alessandro reminded her softly when she failed to reply.

That had been different. She'd been overtired and overwrought and, frankly, freaked out. She wasn't freaked out now. She was something else altogether.

Slowly, irresistibly, she looked at him. Her gaze was instantly ensnared by his. Her breath stalled. So did time. Unable to look away, unable to move, she was intensely aware of the irregular skip of her heart as heat rose. In these last days she'd somehow been restrung inside—

all her senses were working more acutely, making her even more aware of him—of his size, his strength, his scent…his sensuality.

And his sinfully delicious humour.

She'd never met anyone who made her smile the way he did. And all she wanted was to stay near to him. He was a source of fascination and fun and she didn't want to be alone at all any more. She'd had the smallest of tastes on the plane, and now she was starving—*craving* more of that contact.

But she couldn't speak…couldn't ask. Katie had never asked for anything like that in her life. Not intimacy. Nothing personal. And while he'd said he wanted her, he'd wanted lots of women. It didn't make her special in any way.

'Come on. I'll show you the rest.' He abruptly turned and stalked out of the room.

She followed, trying to breathe out and release the tension that tightened every muscle.

The magnificent kitchen provided the perfect distraction. She actually laughed aloud when she realised there were many fantastic appliances to stare at instead of gazing at him.

'Oh, Alessandro, this is gorgeous.'

'You're turned on by my oven?' He leaned back against the marble bench and laughed briefly, only to pause and shoot her a deliberately smouldering glance. 'Good, I'm hungry. Are *you* hungry?'

He's just teasing.

His mouth twitched as she didn't—*couldn't*—reply.

He eventually relented and broke the silence. 'There are vegetables prepared, and fresh fish in the fridge. I'll get on the grill.'

She glanced out of the window and saw a well-planted kitchen garden conveniently near. 'I could find some herbs or something…?'

'Perfect. Run away and hide, *dolcezza*. I'll be waiting here.'

She shot him a look, but left the room. She wasn't going to run and hide—she was going to do what she was good at.

Outside and alone, she sucked in a gulp of fresh summer sea air to clear her head. His effect on her was increasing with every moment and it was mortifying.

Pull it together.

Just because they were married, it didn't mean anything. All that flirtation was just talk—nothing to be taken seriously.

She plucked at plants almost at random, then determinedly walked back into the kitchen, armed with fresh herbs and a wide smile.

'Let me do that.' She moved next to where he stood preparing the fish at the counter.

'You don't have to.'

'Not because I *owe* you—even though I do.' She shook her head at him. 'Because I enjoy it. It relaxes me.'

He put the knife down on the marble counter. 'Well, if you insist…'

She did. It was the perfect way to avoid looking at him and falling deeper beneath his spell. Except he stayed to watch her, and even though she was skilled, it took every ounce of concentration to prepare the food without dicing her fingers in the process.

'I cook every night,' she chatted inanely.

'For Brian?'

'Don't sound so disapproving.' She laughed.

'He takes advantage of you.'

'I'm not a total Cinderella. I love cooking. I do it even when I don't have to...'

When she'd finished plating the food Alessandro stepped forward, putting the plates onto a tray he'd loaded with silverware and glasses. She followed him to the terrace, with its stunning view and sumptuous surroundings. It really was paradise.

'Would you like a drink?'

'Um...'

'I have non-alcoholic.' His eyes twinkled.

'Oh, okay...thank you.' She watched as he poured her a glass, then filled his own from the same bottle. 'Don't let me stop you from—'

'*I'm* stopping me,' he said quietly, but there was steel beneath his soft tone. 'I don't need anything that might take the edge off my resolve.'

Awareness slid like silk over her skin, and for a second she was tempted to throw all caution to the wind and suggest they drink from the other bottle together and then...

But she saved herself from speaking by tucking in to the food she'd prepared. He too seemed to be determined to be distracted by the food.

'You're really good at this, Katie,' he finally said with a satisfied sigh.

She nodded. 'Do you often stay here?' She winced inwardly at her banality. Why couldn't she act like a normal person—not a desperate woman on the edge?

'Ideally for a week or so each month.' A rueful expression flickered across his face and he shrugged. 'Usually not quite a week.'

'Every month?' That was more than she'd expected. 'And you bring people with you?'

Was it party central? Curiosity cut at her, and again she imagined those bikinis by the pool...

His rueful smirk broadened into a real smile and his eyes gleamed, as if he knew what she was really asking. 'No, I prefer peace and quiet when I'm here. I can get a lot of work done.'

'You prefer peace and quiet?' She cocked her head. 'Then you didn't like running that club?'

He'd started his property empire by opening the most popular nightspot in London.

'It was hard work. Late work. But it got me where I needed to be.'

'And where was that?'

'In control. Of my business, my finances, my life.'

Her curiosity deepened. 'You didn't have that control before?'

'It's not always that easy to get, is it?' he said lightly, pointing his fork at her with a teasing look. 'You don't have it. Until today you didn't have any control—'

She stiffened. The edge in his voice raised her defences. 'That—'

'You've been locked away.' He ignored her interruption and spoke faster, the bite of his fury building. 'You should have what you want. Have it *when* you want it. You don't need anyone else's permission or approval. It's your life to live.'

'And that's so easy? Shouldn't I consider other people's feelings at all?' she countered, trying not to get angry in return. 'Or stop to consider that what I want might not actually be all that good for me?'

The thing she wanted right now would *definitely* not be good for her.

He suddenly laughed. 'Ah, you're afraid of getting yourself into trouble...'

He made it sound as if she was a goody-two-shoes, but he didn't understand how important being good had been. She'd have lost everything if she hadn't.

'And you consider other people far too much—at personal cost to yourself,' he added, as if he knew it all.

'Perhaps you don't do it enough?' She couldn't help striking back at him.

'Consider other people's feelings?' He adopted a pious look. 'I'm very careful with other people's feelings.'

'Really?' she muttered sarcastically.

'Are you judging my relationships?'

'Do you even *have* relationships?'

'Sure. Short...sweet. Hot.'

She paused, struck by the honesty underlying that snappy answer.

'Maybe that's not all that good for *you*,' she challenged softly. 'You don't allow yourself to go deeply into relationships so you don't get what's truly good.'

He chuckled, as if she were the most naive creature he'd met. 'I get the good stuff—don't worry about that.'

'There's more to life than good sex, Alessandro.'

'And you would know?' He laughed.

'I might not be experienced in all that—'

'You're so sheltered you've hardly *lived*,' he interrupted with a jeer.

'I've lived a lot, actually,' she argued. 'A great life doesn't always have to mean exotic travel and endless orgasms. Little moments are amazing.'

'How old are you again?' He propped his elbow on the table and pinched the bridge of his nose. 'Are you ready to retire in that orchard?' He shook his head slightly. 'Bury yourself away for all your youth? For heaven's sake, Katie, live a little. You said yourself you don't owe Brian everything—'

'I know that,' she snapped.

'But you're still stuck,' he snapped back. 'Still acting as if you can't break any of his rules.'

She stared at him, silenced. Because he was right.

But she wasn't like Alessandro—not as fiercely independent nor as hedonistic. It wasn't just anyone else's permission or approval that Alessandro refused to need. He refused to *need* anyone in any serious way at all. At least, not for long. It seemed to be his philosophy on life. And good for him.

But she hadn't been entirely useless either, and she resented his implication that she had. 'I *chose* to stay and look after Susan.'

'Of course you did,' he acknowledged. 'But it wasn't like you had any other real option. He'd told you often enough that you owed them.'

Her anger resurged. She hadn't cared for Susan only out of obligation. 'I love her. I *wanted* to…'

She trailed off as his expression altered.

'I know that,' he answered quietly. 'But *Brian* should be the one taking better care of her.'

The bitter note in his voice made a spot in her chest ache. Why was he so bothered by Brian's treatment of his wife?

'Yes, he should,' she acknowledged with a sigh. 'I should have made him.'

'How were you going to do that when—?' Alessandro broke off his too blunt comment and jerked his head in a sharp, negating gesture. 'Naomi didn't take care of my father and I couldn't change that situation either,' he said. 'She and Brian are very alike, unfortunately.'

The curiosity within her deepened into a well. How had Naomi hurt his father? Had things gone wrong before he'd died? Was that why Alessandro had left with so much anger that he'd never returned?

She drew in a breath of courage. 'How—?'

'Do you want to talk to Susan?' he interrupted as he glanced at his watch. 'Now would be a good time.'

She knew he was deliberately diverting her. But she let him. 'Yes, of course. I should have talked to her already.'

'She knows you're okay. Dominique has been in constant contact with her since we married. And she's okay—a nurse companion has started.'

Katie felt guilty all over again. Alessandro had done so much...arranged so much...while she'd just—what? Been unable to think about anything other than him kissing her? She was appalled at her selfishness.

He pulled his phone from his pocket and passed it to her. She quickly tapped in the number.

'Susan?' she said, as soon as her foster mother answered.

'Katie? Is that you?'

'Yes, how are you? Are you okay?'

'Where are you?'

'You're really okay?'

'Is it true?'

Katie half smiled as she realised they were simply firing questions at each other, with neither stopping to answer. She took a breath and slowed down. 'That I've married Alessandro Zetticci? Yes. That's true.'

'I had no idea you'd even seen him since...' Susan drew in an audible breath. 'Why didn't you tell me?'

Katie bit her lip. 'I thought you'd disapprove—'

'Of Alessandro? Is that why you ran away?' Susan sighed. 'I would have talked to Brian. We could have had a lovely ceremony in the gardens...'

Katie slid lower into her seat as relief eased her tension. Susan must be okay if she was able to focus on her precious gardens. She glanced across to Alessandro—clearly he could hear, because her own amusement was mirrored in his eyes.

'I guess we could have...' Katie murmured. 'I'm sorry—'

'Are you happy, Katie?' Susan interrupted.

Katie froze, thrown by her foster mother's serious tone. She'd *thought* she was happy enough at home. She'd been grateful for what she had, and she'd not *let* herself wish for anything more. She'd focused on caring for Susan, on making her sauces, and on the few occasions she'd stopped to think she had hoped that she'd have more eventually. She'd been coping.

But, no, she hadn't been entirely happy. She'd felt constrained by Brian. Following his rules, never feeling good enough, always wary that he would pull the rug from beneath her. As he had when he'd ordered her to marry Carl.

But now she'd had the smallest glimpse of the world beyond White Oaks. Alessandro had done more than enable her—he'd *shown* her. In the few hours she'd been with him she'd done more, seen more, than she had in years. Truthfully, in all her life.

'Katie?' Susan asked her again. 'Are you happy?'

Right this second?

She couldn't look away from the warmth in Alessandro's brilliant blue eyes. Couldn't halt the bubbling sensation in her chest. She could barely answer, but nor could she lie.

'Yes.'

The atmosphere turned electric as the warmth in his eyes was replaced by an indefinable intensity.

Katie swallowed the sudden tightness in her throat and strove to speak. 'I'll be home in a few days. I'll come and see you right away.' Those bubbles fizzed as Alessandro steadily kept watching her. 'Okay?'

'Lovely, darling. I look forward to seeing you both.'

Katie ended the call and handed the phone back to Alessandro, wary of what he might say. More than wary of what he made her feel.

Another flame of guilt licked at her heart. Poor Alessandro. In the last twenty-four hours she'd been demanding and difficult and at times almost rude. But she'd never released her rebellious antagonism towards *anyone* before. It was almost a fire in her blood, pushing her to defy him. To provoke him. She had to settle it somehow.

'Thank you so much for everything,' she said softly.

'I don't want your gratitude,' he snapped. 'That's the last thing I want from you.'

She was transfixed by the blaze in his eyes—not mere warmth, it was blistering. The air thickened, trapping his fierce words between them. One word.

Want.

Her forbidden giveaway reply whispered out. 'What *do* you want from me?'

Heat rose in her cheeks as her mind raced with every intimate possibility her inexperienced self could think of. Her heart skipped, and then skidded to a sprint that left breathing impossible.

But Alessandro slowly shook his head. 'No,' he said harshly, his gaze not lifting from hers. 'You're not transferring your need to people-please to me.'

Katie flinched, because she'd been strung out waiting for his reply. For those few moments she'd been willing to let him do anything he wanted. And that was mortifying. Because he didn't want her. Not really. He had been playing with her on the plane, because she was inexperienced and it was mildly entertaining for him.

'Sex is always a game.'

The worst thing was that he knew what she'd been thinking. He could read her mind as easily as a front-page headline.

He suddenly pushed back from the table and stood in a jerky moment. 'You owe me *nothing*—understand?'

CHAPTER EIGHT

ALESSANDRO STALKED TO the kitchen and tossed their plates into the dishwasher. He'd insisted he didn't want her help because he needed ten minutes alone to get himself together.

Except the kitchen was now tainted with echoes of her scent and sound and the sight of her at that bench.

She'd relaxed in here, swiftly preparing dinner with skill, her smile small and private while she focused intently on her task.

He'd been almost unable to do anything other than stare at her. He'd been staring at her pretty much all afternoon. He was still recovering from the bronze bikini that had brought out the amber lights in her eyes.

Those three guys by the pool had liked it too. She hadn't appeared to notice them, but Alessandro sure as hell had seen them eating her with their eyes. Protective—*possessive*—he'd pointedly wrapped his arm around her, leaving them in no doubt she was taken.

His jealousy, his loss of control over his own body, horrified him. She made him feel as if he'd been starved of sex for centuries. Which he hadn't. Yet he was struggling to control the urge to touch her. His desire burned hotter than an exploding supernova.

Her hair was no longer in that low ponytail, but hung loose and shining after her trip to the salon earlier today. He was glad she hadn't cut much of the length. It gleamed a gorgeous brown, flecked with strands of gold—a myriad of colours to match her eyes.

The dress she'd chosen was bolder than he'd expected—a bright splash of summer colour with a fit that emphasised her narrow waist. He wanted to rip the pretty thing off her like some lust-crazed monster. The longer he was around her, the stronger that wildness within him grew. But it wasn't her new haircut or the clothing that had made the difference. It was her blossoming confidence, that lick of awareness, the anticipation in her eyes.

The memory of her response.

Kissing her had been a massive mistake. He'd discovered too much that was tempting—her sweetness, her heat, her innate passion. And he didn't think he could resist it. He who could walk away from anything—anyone—had had to *run* from her.

She'd infected him—injected a fever into his veins. Now the fever was spreading and all he wanted was *more*. All he could think about was her.

He left the kitchen and walked along the terrace, stopping at the balustrade overlooking the pool. He didn't notice the view, or the scent of the summer flowers, or the warmth of the evening air. He was too busy stopping himself from going to find her.

He was deluding himself that he'd just talk to her—talking to her was oddly easy. But that set another alarm off. He didn't talk to his lovers. He gave pleasure. Took pleasure. And then left.

But he'd had to bite back talking more about Naomi and his father. Of all things that was the one he never discussed with anyone, and yet he'd been so close to telling Katie every silly little thing—even his personal history with this island too…

But he needed to maintain the distance between them because soon enough they'd separate.

He gripped the railing with both hands. He shouldn't have brought her here. It was his private space. But he'd thought he'd be able to prepare her for the charade they were to play for the next few months here—get her over the wobbles. Instead *he* was the one on edge, struggling for self-control, almost consumed by temptation when he knew he shouldn't take advantage of her.

But she's using you.

She wanted his help, his money, his power…for protection. For him to seduce her in return would be too much of a personal price for her to pay, even if she was willing. And if he were any kind of a decent human being he wouldn't even consider it.

But she wants you too.

She hadn't just responded when he'd kissed her—she'd ignited. Sure, there had been some gratitude mixed up in it, but there had been raw, red-hot desire for him there too. He was experienced enough to know that. What was more, the carnal curiosity in her eyes brightened with every interaction they had.

And it was killing him—death by temptation. Maybe they could indulge just a *little*…?

He twisted his lips at that devil inside, tearing him apart, and at his confusion. Why did she captivate him so completely? He'd had plenty of women—all more classically beautiful, more successful, certainly more experienced…

He glared into the blue water. Her virginity wasn't

what aroused him… That appallingly inconvenient little fact was the complication that made having her impossible.

Gritting his teeth, he gripped the railing so tight his knuckles turned white.

'Alessandro?'

He turned towards her voice. She warily walked nearer, watching him the way a zoo-keeper might watch a pacing barely caged tiger.

'Mmm?' He tightened his grip to stop himself grabbing her.

'Are you okay?'

'No,' he muttered bluntly, unable to lie because he was tired and too tightly wired to hold back—at least verbally. 'Not okay.'

He'd never struggled with his self-control before.

He'd never wanted one woman with this intensity before.

'Anything I can do?'

Oh, of *course* she'd offer to help, wouldn't she? So willing and eager to please. Which was exactly what he wanted and yet everything he didn't, all at the same time.

Her expression dimmed and a frown slowly formed. 'If you're in a mood I'll leave you to your thoughts.'

Again, everything he wanted and didn't want.

'You confuse me,' he ground out. 'Or rather my feelings for you confuse me.'

She reached out for the railing beside him and held on as tightly as he was. 'You have feelings for me?'

He cleared his throat, grimacing at his uncustomary clumsiness. He did not struggle to think around women.

And he never let them wonder what he wanted or definitely *didn't* want from them.

'Perhaps urges would be a better word.'

He heard a soft gasp and her bubbling laugh warmed the air. 'Oh. *Those.*'

'You have them too?' He shot her a sideways look, unable to stop his own small smile.

As her gaze meshed with his her laugh dissolved into a sigh. 'I'm trying to ignore them.' She bit her lip.

'Why?' *And how?*

'To prove to myself that I can.'

He frowned. Why did she need to do that? She'd been so sheltered, and she seemed far too focused on self-control. Alessandro knew that life was short, and Katie seemed to have spent all of hers so far trying to please other people. Why couldn't she just please herself for once?

That temptation spiralled. He knew that her pleasing herself would definitely please him.

'Okay, so how are you going to reward yourself?' He released the railing and moved closer to her. He simply couldn't resist any more. 'Once you've proved your self-control?'

Her eyes widened with every step he took. Her quickened breath was gratifying. Maybe it wasn't as easy as all that for her to ignore those urges.

His body tightened in response and readiness. Damn this restraint. He was sick of trying to be a goddamn hero—it wasn't a natural fit. In the school of life he was a player, not a prefect.

'How am I going to...*what*?' she asked breathlessly.

He smiled at her distraction. 'Going to reward yourself?' He stopped right beside her. 'It seems to me that you're very good at doing what others ask of you. You're very good at keeping yourself in check. Very good at doing what you need to.' Or not doing what she thought she shouldn't. 'So how do you reward *yourself*?'

She didn't—that was obvious.

'The reward is in the action,' she said, her nose wrinkling, as if she were confused by his question. 'By doing—or in this case *not* doing—I feel good.'

Did she really? He didn't think so. He thought she felt as achy and restless as he did. She was watching him too keenly, her whole body was strained. And, heaven help him, he could see the sharp outline of her nipples against the pretty fabric of her dress.

'But it isn't going away, Katie. In fact, it's only getting worse.' Which was intensely unusual for him.

Her luminous eyes widened. 'Are you suggesting that my reward for *not* tangling with you should be for me to tangle with you?'

'You don't actually have to do anything.' He reached out to run his hand the length of her shining hair. It was a beacon he could no longer ignore. 'You can just lie there and take your reward, *dolcezza*.'

He wanted her on a bed—writhing, welcoming, arching in ecstasy. What he'd do to make her scream… She'd be so beautiful.

Sheer shock immobilised her, and then desire glazed her eyes. 'Alessandro…'

It was a caution. But it was also shy need.

And it was surrender.

He wrapped his arm around her waist and pulled her to him. He stared down at her, reading her expression, the softness and the sensual tension in her body. She put her hands on his chest—but not to push away.

In fact she arched nearer. Her lips parted on a pout, her breathing hitched. She wanted to touch as much as he did. She was every bit as willing.

'Let me be your reward,' he dared her huskily.

'I'm afraid you're my poison,' she shivered. But her hands slid up his chest, shyly exploring. 'You're such temptation...'

He shook his head, leaning closer, his body aching for her fingers to skim further. 'That's *you.*'

'You can turn any woman on,' she moaned. 'It's so unfair.'

'If you like I can give you some pointers.'

She half laughed and looked down, letting the fall of her hair hide her face.

He cupped her chin and made her look up into his eyes. 'I'm not going to apologise for my past, Katie. But you must know this kind of chemistry doesn't happen every day. It's rare. And seemingly almost impossible to restrain.'

'You're just saying that...' she mumbled.

'No, I'm not. But even so it's still just nothing...' he whispered, brushing closer to her. *It was always nothing.*

'Can something this intense be just nothing?' she asked.

He groaned at what her question gave away. He didn't answer. He couldn't. All he could do now was succumb to the savage need to kiss her. He'd show, not tell.

Intense, yes. Nothing, yes.

His relief at her immediate response lasted mere seconds before restraint became almost impossible. Her lips were luscious and pillowy and so sweet. He tried to ease back so he didn't bruise her, but he heard her little moan of outrage and felt her rise on tiptoes to keep him close. And instead of easing back he slipped his leash—smashing his lips on hers, almost brutal in his possession.

And she met him, matched him. Her hands slid around to his back and held him tighter. Her tongue lashed against his...her breasts pressed close to his chest. He lost his breath, lost his reason. He was unable to resist deepening everything—taking them swiftly to a desperation beyond anything even he'd felt.

Desire combusted. He ought to release her and run—lock himself away until he had himself under control again. But he ached to hear her scream and see her sated—to see the smile of satisfaction on her lips. Determination flared as he felt her trembling need and the tight clasp of her fingers on his shirt. He could control himself enough to see her release. He could make this about her. It was the only acceptable outcome now.

'It's only a moment, Katie.' He was reminding himself as much as reassuring her. 'Only to ease the ache.'

He picked her up and carried her through the open doors before reason could return. He gently placed her in the centre of her big bed, determined not to take everything. He'd not give in to the urge to claim her completely. Not for him that ultimate pleasure. Not with her. She deserved more than he could ever offer her.

But he could give her something. He kissed her, swept away by all the sensations of touching and tasting her—all caramel and honey, silken warm curves. He didn't undress—not himself, nor her. It was the only way to maintain his control. Because in those kisses he'd felt her shivering surrender.

She softened, her legs spreading, offering more than

she could possibly realise. He couldn't resist cupping her. Fury swamped him as he felt her damp heat through the thin barrier of her panties.

'How dare you deny yourself when you're this hot?' he rasped. 'Why do you hold back from something you really want?'

He was oddly furious, because this was about more than this moment with him now. This was about her whole life. She'd denied herself so much.

'You should have what you want,' he told her roughly, bending to tend to her hungry mouth. 'You should always have what you want. What you deserve.'

He wanted to see her undone...all the way to completion. He hated the way she treated herself. As if she believed she didn't deserve more.

She trembled as he strummed her lightly and kissed her hard. She moaned into his mouth, her body rippling beneath his. He lifted his head and stared at her. They'd barely started and she'd ignited. So on the edge. So needy. She'd been restrained too long...as if she were afraid to have her voice heard.

He wanted to hear her voice—her scream. It shot him to the edge too. He wanted time to cease so he could hang in this moment, where he had her where he wanted her—spread before him, hot and wet and willing. He choked on his own groan, holding back as he felt her full-bodied feminine response to his touch.

She was so supple, sweet, eager. Her scent, her warmth, all her responses were beautiful. His body tightened to the point of pain, and the urge to claim and conquer almost overpowered him. He was close to losing his head. But it was imperative to him that she should feel maximum pleasure. This time the desire to please was all his.

Focus only on her. Utterly on her.

Katie gasped, struggling to hold herself together. She shouldn't just lie here…she should touch him back… But what he was doing felt too good, and the reckless desire consuming her was uncontrollable. The ache was so much more than she could handle. She couldn't deny herself, couldn't make herself move—too scared to in case he stopped. She wanted his touch more than she'd ever wanted anything. And he knew it.

He let out a low little laugh—the sexiest sound she'd ever heard—and teased and stoked the flames higher. He kissed her with fierce passion, only to ease back again, roving leisurely down her neck to nibble along the neckline of her dress. Her breasts tightened, wanting some of his attention. But his hands swept down her sides, lifting the silk dress to skim across her thighs.

She sighed, lifting her hips as he sought out her secrets, guiding her along a rapid current of heat and want. Her lips felt hot and a little swollen, and all she wanted was for him to kiss her again—to tease his tongue inside her mouth the way he had before. She ached for the weight of him above her, for him to pin her down and fix her in place with his powerful body.

She couldn't say it, couldn't ask. She could only clutch the sheet beneath her to help hold back her screams.

He lifted his head to look down at her with those smouldering eyes. 'I dare you to do what you want, say what you want—to take what you want, when you want it.' His words were slightly slurred and his strokes up her inner thigh quickened.

'You don't think I've done that already?'

She circled her hips again on pure instinct, wanting him to go higher, wanting more to the point of madness. Wanting it enough to be provoked into answering with all the rebellion she'd normally deny herself.

'Are we not now married because I was ballsy enough to ask you?'

'You were compelled to do that because you wanted to protect Susan.' He stroked her higher, faster, and lowered his head until his mouth was tantalisingly close to hers. 'But you didn't want to marry anyone. Not Carl. Not me either. You did what you thought you had to, for someone else. When did you last do something for yourself?'

He was teasing, tormenting, pushing her, whispering provocation against her lips.

Silently she stared up at him and pushed her legs a little further apart, granting him unrestricted access. Wordlessly telling him what she wanted.

He slid his hand higher, almost to where she ached most.

'You don't do it often enough,' Alessandro growled. 'What do you want, Katie? *Tell* me.'

'Kiss me,' she whispered in a breathless rush.

In an instant her wish was granted. His kiss was carnal and hot, and at the exact moment his tongue plundered her mouth his fingers teased her secret, most sensitive spot. It took only that stroke and suddenly all the fireworks in the world exploded within her.

She screamed as intense convulsions radiated from where he cupped her core. She twisted in his arms but he didn't release her. His mouth moved to her neck, kissing her while his fingers kept up the delicious torture that tore her into nothing but shreds of sensation.

'So hot. So quick.' A soft exultant laugh followed the last echo of her cries. 'You can't tell me you didn't need that.'

She couldn't answer because she couldn't move. She couldn't see how she was ever going to recover from something that felt so good.

He gently caressed her, keeping her close until the orgasmic quivers began to ease. She felt boneless, weightless, as if she were floating along a warm river of bliss. She opened her eyes and looked straight into his.

The remnants of his smile faded as he gazed down at her until lines of tension bracketed his mouth. When she arched her back just a little his jaw clenched. And as he lost the battle to mask his strain a new energy coiled within her—embers to spark that driving desire.

Not enough.

The sharp knife of need sliced through the last vestige of her relief.

More.

It should have been impossible—only a moment ago she'd experienced an intense orgasm, the most intimate embrace of her life. But he'd roused a hunger she'd never known she had, nor that she was capable of. She needed to know—to share all of herself with him and have him with her...*in* her. What he'd just done wasn't enough, and she had not done enough.

But at the exact moment she realised that he pushed away from her, vaulting off the bed.

'Where are you going?' His vehement speed had shocked the question out of her.

'Out. Before I do something I promised us both that I wouldn't.'

'Alessandro—'

'No.' He shook his head.

Her heart pounded. 'But you…' She trailed off, unable to say it. He hadn't had the release she'd had.

His lips twisted as he read her expression. 'I'll survive.'

'But—'

He stepped forward with a swift movement and pressed his hands into the mattress either side of her head, as if he didn't trust himself to touch her again.

'Don't.'

'But—'

With a growl he bent and caught her mouth in a kiss. She melted, opening to let him in, curling her tongue around his hungrily, the way he'd taught her. But too soon he tore away, with a choked noise in the back of his throat.

He didn't speak until he got to the door. Even then he didn't look back.

'Sweet dreams, Katie.'

CHAPTER NINE

IT WAS IMPOSSIBLE to relax, to forget, to deny, because the bone-deep satisfaction didn't stay—instead bitterness and confusion built.

But worst of all was the desire. It surged more powerful than ever, pacing within her like a creature of the wild, caged in a prison too small. It strengthened with every unstoppable memory—every caress, every kiss that she couldn't forget—until finally it morphed into a fire of frustration that flashed through her system, rendering sleep impossible.

After a few burning restless hours she gave up trying. Needing to cool down, she walked out through the open doorway from her bedroom to the courtyard. The moon cast a silvery path on the darkened water and in the far distance moored boats gleamed in the moonlight. Gentle waves lapped against the beach below.

'You can't sleep?'

His low query didn't startle her. Somehow she'd known he'd be out here too.

And of *course* she couldn't sleep.

Alessandro was sitting at the table where they'd dined, his expression indecipherable in the shadows. But his tone held an edge of mockery. Her frustration flared but she refused to react. She wasn't going to try to provoke him again. She was ignoring that shameless, wilful part of herself.

'It's beautiful,' she murmured, turning back to the water and trying to think of something innocuous to mask her inner turmoil. 'No wonder you come here as often as you can.'

Her tension pulled tighter when he didn't reply. She wrapped her arms around her waist, even though her new silk nightdress was already too hot. She was conscious of her breathing, aware of the distance between them, of the thrum of desire beating relentlessly in her veins.

She finally looked from the water back to him. She could see the gorgeous gleam of his eyes but couldn't read anything in it. Earlier he'd left her so easily. Which meant he'd not really wanted her. It hadn't even been a game for him, so why had he…?

She couldn't hold back the question. 'Alessandro—?'

'Go back to bed, Katie,' he forestalled her huskily.

'No.'

'Katie…'

She hated that tone. 'You don't want my gratitude?' She tossed her head proudly. 'Then I don't want your pity.'

'Pardon?' A thread of molten steel had entered his voice.

Power flowed through her veins. Control. Pride. Dignity. *This* was what she needed to do. She needed to tell him what she *didn't* want.

'Don't do me any more favours.'

'Is that what you think that was?' He pushed back

from the table, his chair scraping loudly on the flag-stones. 'I can't—'

'You don't want to,' she snapped.

'Katie—' His muttered oath rubbished her accusation. 'There's no going back.'

Her anger sparked at his hesitation, at his treatment of her as a naive fool. 'You told me to ask for what I wanted. I finally did. But then you walked away.'

He stood, planted his feet wide and stared at her like a determined statue. Too damned heroic.

'I've been regretting it ever since.'

He regretted stopping? Excitement roared through her at his response.

'Be very sure about your next move, *dolcezza*. Because if you ask again I'll say yes. And I won't leave. Not until we're both done.'

Could she be this selfish—take more from him?

'But I can't give you everything you want,' he added harshly. 'I'll never be able to do that.'

'How do you know everything I want?' she replied, her spirits rising. 'I've never said I wanted "everything" from you. I just want *now* with you. Just for me.'

He remained motionless and unyielding.

She stared at the fierce intensity in his eyes. 'I can make up my own mind!' Katie's frustration at his unnecessary protectiveness exploded. 'I don't need *you* to make the decision for me.'

His breath hissed out between clenched teeth. 'No? You're claiming control? Fine.' He took one barely leashed step forward. 'But some elements I *do* get to decide.'

The steel in his voice sent a shock of anticipation

into that secret part of her—so thrilling, so stunning, she was rendered speechless.

'My room. My bed. My way.'

He punctuated each word with another step towards her.

She couldn't move, locked in place by the burn of blue. He was so strong, so consuming, and as he stalked closer she felt the overwhelming desire to surrender— to simply melt before him. *This* was what she wanted. His attention. Nothing but now. All physical.

She closed her mind to the complications of the future, not even daring to consider the next five minutes. She couldn't bear the agony of embarrassment.

She chose just him—just now. 'Okay.'

He swallowed and took the last step towards her. In the moonlight she saw the faintest sheen of sweat skimming his skin. He wore only boxers, and they did little to hide the reaction of his body. For a moment she just stared, her heart thudding with a roar of both anticipation and anxiety, before she made herself look away.

Her knees weakened as desire rushed to pool low in her belly. But with his all-seeing eyes he knew she'd peeked.

'Not pity,' he teased softly. 'You're getting something far more powerful than pity, Katie.'

That old playboy arrogance was tinder to the spark of rebellion that smoked only in his presence. To the need to fire back at him.

Her heart quadrupled its pace. She ran her tongue over her parched lips but was barely able to mutter the response that he'd provoked. 'Prove it.'

His lips curved, but that sly smile didn't soften the

steeliness in his eyes. 'Next time you dare me, try taking a breath first.'

'It's impossible to breathe around you,' she confessed.

His hand cupped her jaw. 'Katie...'

For a horrible moment she thought he was going to deny her. But then he bent towards her. His kiss tasted of lemon and mint, cool and refreshing. His body brushed against hers, his skin burning through her silk slip. She uncurled her fists, reaching out to touch him, resting her hands on his waist. The kiss deepened. Emboldened, she traced more of his skin, discovering his strength and height and heat.

His muscles tensed beneath her touch and he tore his lips from hers. 'Katie—inside.' He paused and then stepped back.

He didn't reach to pick her up and carry her this time. Instinctively she knew he was testing her, ensuring that this was her choice, her decision. Her legs trembled—but not from fear. It was anticipation...pure yearning.

This once, she promised herself. There was no one else she wanted—that she'd ever wanted. He was a present to herself in this fantasy place for this one perfect night. She couldn't deny herself and she'd have no regrets.

His bedroom was even more vast than hers. The curtains weren't drawn and in the bright moonlight the spacious bed gleamed—a pearled place for private pleasure. She noticed the white coverings were untouched—had he not even tried to sleep tonight?

Her pulse thundered as she sat on the bed. Her senses were so heightened that the luxurious linen felt deliciously soft and cool on her overly sensitive skin. He didn't move to join her. Did she have to ask him again?

But then he released a harsh breath and came to her. As he knelt on the bed beside her he framed her face in his hands and kissed her hard and deep and long. She tumbled into the sensation—all sweet heat and relief—because finally she was here, with him, having what she wanted…needed…from him. With nothing held back.

He lifted his head and took his time. To her infinite torment he touched her slowly, slipping the thin straps of her soft silk nightgown from her shoulders. Then he tugged it lower, exposing her breasts to his gaze. To his touch. To his kiss. Then he pulled the gown lower still, until she was bared completely. He paused and cocked his head, one hand rubbing the back of his neck as he surveyed her with hungry eyes.

'You're beautiful,' he muttered hoarsely, and bent to kiss her belly, then to kiss her lower still.

'You don't have to flatter me…' she moaned, turning her head to press her cheek to the cool sheet, briefly closing her eyes at the intensity of such an intimate touch.

'Don't hide behind your judgemental ideas of me to reject my appreciation,' he growled, lifting his head and waiting until she turned and looked him in the eyes. 'Accept the compliment, Katie.' He placed his hand on her—intimately. 'Accept the caress. Or we cannot continue.'

His gaze, his touch, burned into her—through her—until she had no recourse but to release the pent-up tension in a deep sigh and slide her legs a little further apart.

'Yes,' she whispered.

'Good…' He smiled. 'Because I need to see you. I need to taste you. I need to have you.'

His words shook a fierce response from her, and his hands stoked it even higher. His fingertips swept over her and his mouth followed, bestowing caresses and kisses both firm and gentle, playful and passionate. All the length of her body sensation ignited—blissful pleasure and a desperate, driving need for more.

He chuckled as she arched, to encourage him to stroke harder, to touch her right where she was so tormented. But he didn't. He held back with deliberate devastation.

'Not yet.' His words sounded slightly slurred as he shifted and began again.

He teased her to the brink and back again. Once, twice…until she was writhing, shaking and finally asking all over again—begging, in fact. She couldn't take it any more.

'Please, Alessandro…'

He smiled that wonderful, wicked, infuriating smile that always made her tumble towards him. And then he moved closer, kissing her lower, then lower, while his hand cupped and his finger teased.

She shivered as he discovered her hot, wet secrets. Slowly, gently, he slid a single finger inside her. She moved uncontrollably, then tensed as a moment of lucidity hit—as she realised the total intimacy of his touch.

'Let yourself go,' he breathed against her. 'Your instincts are good.'

She had no choice but to obey the dictates of her trembling, aching body, because then he sealed his mouth to that most sensual private part of her. She arched, driving her hips high against him, and screamed in ecstasy as he relentlessly subjected her to the most intimate, most incredible experience of her life.

The orgasm shot through her, racking every muscle and cell, twisting her inside out in a series of pleasurable pulses, until she finally fell back on the bed in a limp heap. But even as she breathed out that last sigh of supreme delight she realised her body was charged—fully powered and ready for something so much more. Something she instinctively knew only he could give her.

He lifted himself right away from her.

Shocked, she watched him stand. 'Seriously…?'

He shot her a look—tension intertwined with amusement. 'Absolutely.'

She realised he'd retrieved a box from the drawer in the small table beside the bed. Her heart thudded as he finally removed the boxers that had been the only barrier between them and rolled a condom down his length.

Katie ran her tongue along her lip and then swallowed—unable to look away, unable to speak.

'I'll take care of you, Katie,' he said softly.

But that steely determination was still audible.

It made her shiver. 'I know.'

The moment he came back to her on the bed the chemistry between them combusted. He gently nudged her legs apart with his, bracing himself over her and kissing her beyond anticipation all over again. He was so, so close, and she'd never been as excited, as aching, in all her life.

But then he paused to look deep into her eyes. 'Are you—?'

She twisted beneath him in an agony of desire. 'Don't you *dare* ask me again.'

He half laughed, but she could see the strain around

his eyes. She put her hand on his jaw, feeling the heat of his skin, the sheen of sweat covering him.

'Katie...' He cupped her face in return, then slid his fingers to lace them through her hair. His eyes locked on hers. 'You're beautiful,' he said. 'More beautiful than is comfortable,' he added in an almost inaudible murmur.

He pressed closer. She drew in a shocked, sharp breath, her eyes fluttering shut as she strained to take him.

His low groan felled her. 'Katie... Breathe.'

She trembled, yielding on a soft sigh as he pushed right inside her. He was so big, his invasion hard and thick, and now he paused, searching her eyes as he slowly took what she offered and gave what she needed.

Silently they stared at each other as he pressed ever so slightly closer, sliding deeper into her tight, slick body. She moaned at the sensation—so full, so overwhelming. And just at the moment when she thought it was too much he kissed her—tenderly, but taking her totally. His tongue caressed her slow and deep, matching the rhythm of his hips, pressing close and then releasing before thrusting closer, then closer again.

She more than melted. She moved—breaking free of his kiss to gasp in delight and arch closer as she suddenly realised just how good this was.

'That's it,' he muttered, bearing down on her again. 'Take me.'

His hand swept lower, his fingers teasing the secret place where they were pressed close. She felt his rigid length deep inside, stroking her. It felt so good. Her mouth parted as her breathing became erratic and moans of excitement escaped. Her gaze was locked on his. She felt his determination, his approval as she tumbled deeper into a vortex of intensity where heat and darkness coalesced.

She cried out again as pleasure swept over her in a great wave. She wound her arms tight around him and literally rode him through it—the cause of her pleasure and her anchor through the storm of sensation.

And then…when she finally returned to calm…she refused to release him. She held his roughened jaw between her palms, looking right into his eyes.

His smile slipped a little. 'Katie…' Half warning, half praise. 'You okay?'

She nodded. She could hardly speak for the intensity of her satisfaction. She simply sighed his name. 'Alessandro…'

He smiled, then kissed her as if he was pouring his soul into her. 'A little more,' he whispered. 'Just a little more. Okay?'

'Yes.'

It was more than okay. She didn't want this to end. She hadn't had everything yet. She hadn't had him shaking in her arms the way she'd shaken in his.

He smiled as he watched her, apparently able to read her mind. 'Come with me this time.'

It should have been impossible. The orgasm she'd just enjoyed had been so intense. Only his words triggered a lick of electricity that she recognised. She felt the heat and damp of his skin, the tension holding him fiercely still as he locked against her and her own desire surged. She wanted him to let go too.

Primal instinct kicked in and her body took over. She curled her leg around his waist, locking him deeper to her, and slid her arms more tightly around his back.

'Your instincts are good,' he'd assured her. And he was right. Because this felt even better.

The look in his blue eyes became even more brilliant. 'Katie—'

'More, Alessandro. Please.' She'd loved all his tenderness, but she wanted his passion too.

With a groan he pressed his hands beside her, levering himself up so he could drive deeper into her. This wasn't pleasure. This was beyond anything that could be defined that simply.

Her lips parted as she panted with every pounding thrust. She squeezed him with her arms and legs, aching to hold him more tightly, more deeply inside her. She couldn't get close enough. She *still* couldn't get close enough.

'Katie…' he choked. 'Katie…' He lapsed into unintelligible Italian.

This was what she wanted.

This was even better than before.

The ripple took her by surprise, tearing through her, seizing every muscle, making her fingers like claws that dug into him. And he was the same with her—buried to the hilt and then some. Rammed together—clutching, kissing, totally connected—they shared every inch, every sensation.

'I had no idea…' she gasped.

It wasn't a trickle of goodness. It was a river—a shimmering cascade of delight spreading throughout her body and beyond. Seeping into him too, into this bubble they'd created. This cocoon of such intimacy, such connection.

She'd never felt as close to anyone. Never felt as secure. Even if it was only for these few moments, it was the best feeling of her life.

'Thank you.'

'Katie…' The lightest puff of teasing disapproval.

She couldn't summon the energy to open her eyes, but she smiled a little sadly. 'I mean it.'

He held her close and rolled, lifting her to lie on his chest. He cradled her as the last shivers of delight skimmed her skin.

'Thank *you*.' He released a long, satisfied sigh.

She'd not expected words of love—of course she hadn't. But now she felt their absence. It was an alarmingly vast emptiness that ached.

That 'everything' she'd said she didn't want from him…?

No.

She refused to recognise the extent of that yearning. This would only be a temporary pleasure. That was what it was for him. This gnawing feeling inside was simply lust all over again. Purely physical. She'd be satisfied with his body, his skill, and she'd have her fill of him.

And now, impossibly, when she'd been exhausted only moments ago, she was energised again.

'Katie?'

Of course he'd sensed it.

His hands tightened on her waist and he shifted, sliding her beneath him.

'Show me more,' she said, and kissed him before he could answer, desperately drowning the doubt that was trying to curl its cold tendrils around her heart.

Oh, Katie, what have you done?

CHAPTER TEN

TROUBLE SLITHERED LIKE a clever snake, avoiding detection until it was too late to stop its strike. While last night had been wonderful, it had also been dangerous. More than she'd thought possible.

Katie showered beneath cold water, desperate to settle the confusing thoughts and feelings swirling in her head. It was just sex. Natural. Normal. Nothing profound. Nothing out of the ordinary. Yet her heart pounded. Instinctively she knew her response was more intense than 'normal'. *Her instincts were good*, and they were right on this.

This wasn't some 'people-pleasing' problem like Alessandro had teased her about. She'd been utterly unable to resist the temptation of him last night, and this morning that impulse was even stronger. She'd naively thought it would have eased. Wasn't that what happened when you scratched an itch? It went away. It wasn't supposed to itch more. Lots of people had casual flings or one-night stands and moved on.

Only she'd sunk deeper into the pool of infatuation. Truthfully, she was halfway to falling for him completely. He'd helped her. He'd listened. He'd been kind. But he also challenged her constantly, while invariably making her laugh at the same time, and that just made him magnetic. Add the way he could please her physically and she stood no chance.

She mocked herself for being sentimental—for weaving fairy tales into her fantasies. As a lonely teen she'd dreamt of being swept off her feet and being ravished, of being taken away to some wondrous kingdom where she was safe and secure and *loved* for all time…

But Alessandro wasn't Prince Charming. There was no happy-ever-after in his world. This was only fun—moments that meant nothing. Last night had been merely that for him, and while she knew that he'd truly wanted her, soon enough he wouldn't.

Already that thought terrified her more than it ought. Because she knew too well how being unwanted hurt.

She had to protect herself—she had to be stronger. He'd told her to take what she wanted, but how could she when she knew she was putting herself at risk?

He'd also wanted honesty…and that she could give him. She'd grown some courage in the last couple of days. She could do what she *needed* to do—what was best for *her*.

Alessandro sat out on the terrace and scrolled through his emails, trying to distract himself while waiting for Katie to emerge. He'd slept late, but when he'd woken she'd still been in a deep slumber and he'd not wanted to disturb her, despite the ache in his gut tempting him to touch her.

Grimly he put the tablet on the table, giving up on any semblance of concentration on work. He shouldn't have said yes to her, but he'd been powerless to say no when he'd wanted her more than he'd wanted anyone.

Unfortunately, he still did.

His skin tightened at the merest recollection. Unease tensed his muscles even more. Her lack of experience and her lonely upbringing made her vulnerable. Yet she'd teased him that he didn't go into relationships deeply enough. Why would he need to when he'd never intended to get married? But now he had—and he didn't want to hurt her. Somehow he needed to keep this from getting more complicated.

He gritted his teeth, because the obvious way was by shutting down the physical aspect of their relationship. Except all he wanted was to get back into bed with her.

'Good morning.'

He glanced up at her soft greeting and couldn't help smiling as colour flooded her face as she walked towards where he sat. There wasn't a part of her he hadn't kissed and yet she still blushed. He hungered to peel off her clothes and see that flush over all her skin. Right now.

No.

He lifted the coffee pot and poured her a cup. 'How are you?' He tried to keep it light, but tension tightened his throat.

'Good.' She accepted the coffee, keeping her gaze on the cup and not him. 'Sorry I slept so late.'

'You needed it.'

He coughed out the huskiness in his voice. He hated it that she still apologised and felt she needed to explain her behaviour all the time.

She kept her eyes averted. Wariness prickled down his spine. Already he knew that look. She had something on her mind. That made two of them.

'What's up?' he prompted.

She sipped her drink, bracing herself as if nervous. 'I've been thinking…'

'Sounds dangerous,' he teased when she trailed off. 'You have another crazy plan in your head?'

A small smile crossed her lips and she nodded.

He drew in an exaggerated breath. 'Okay, hit me with it.'

She hesitated, her glance skittering away from him again. 'I just want you to know I had a great time last night…'

He narrowed his gaze, all senses suddenly on full alert.

'But I don't think…'

His brain sharpened as she trailed off again. Was she attempting her first 'one-night-and-walk-away'—her first ever break-up? Her thinking was more dangerous than he'd imagined.

'We shouldn't do that again,' she said quickly.

'Do what again?' He wanted to make her spell it out. Wanted to make her blush awkwardly all over again. Because he was feeling oddly wounded.

'We shouldn't sleep together,' she said more firmly.

'You mean have sex?'

'That too.'

He blinked. *Wow.* Even though it was exactly what *he'd* been thinking less than five minutes ago, now the idea seemed like pure madness. Had he disappointed her in some way? He refused to believe it.

'I made you—'

'Yes,' she blurted, interrupting him. 'I had too good a time.'

Was that even possible? He relaxed a little and

rubbed his hand across his mouth to hide his smile. 'So the problem is…?'

'It's simple pleasure to you,' she said, straightening. 'You said it's just a fun pastime. And I can see why… It's amazing.'

He dropped his hand and stared at her warily.

'The thing is…' She paused to cough the frog from her throat and sent him an apologetic smile. 'I think it might not be that simple for me. I liked it…too much. I know it's probably just because…you know…I'm not that experienced and you're really—'

He held up his hand to stop her. 'I can't make out if you're insulting me or paying me a compliment.'

'You're really good at making a woman feel good,' she said earnestly, regardless of his interruption. 'The problem is if you keep making me feel that good I'll probably end up fancying myself in love with you.'

'And of course that is beyond the realms of possibility?' He forced a smile past the hollowness in his chest. 'Once again, I thank you for your honesty.'

'It's just better if we don't sleep together again.' She held the coffee cup close to her chest.

'One night really was enough for you?' Rebellion bubbled in his blood. 'Straight back to self-denial, Katie?'

She'd scuttled into her box, hiding away when she didn't have to. He was tempted to stand up and take the two steps to get close to her again. One kiss and he'd convince her otherwise.

'Self-preservation,' she corrected quietly.

'Are you trying to scare me off?' he asked, attempting a small tease when in fact he felt the furthest from laughing he'd felt in years.

'I'm not like you…' she breathed. 'I don't want to be just another lover for anyone,' she said.

He rubbed his forehead. 'I'm not the complete playboy you seem to think I am.' His gaze narrowed when he saw the disbelieving arch of her eyebrows. 'I played that up because you were being so judgey. How do you think I got my clubs so damn popular? It was all part of the image.'

She shook her head at him, her eyes serious. 'No, Alessandro. I *saw* you.'

He paused. 'Saw me what?'

Her blush deepened. 'You were about eighteen…it wasn't long before you left White Oaks for the last time. I saw you in the orchard. You were…entertaining one of the summer workers. A few days later you were entertaining another. You've *always* had lots of women. It wasn't about building your business then.'

'You saw me "entertaining" one of the student workers? What was I doing?' He racked his brain, trying to remember who or when, but honestly that period in his life had been hideous.

She didn't reply but that flush under her skin deepened in colour. Clearly he'd been doing a little more than kissing a girl.

'Did you like watching me?' he asked roughly.

Her eyes widened in surprise and the colour mottled all down her neck. 'I was only… I didn't know what I was watching.'

Definitely more than just kissing. He gazed at her searchingly, compelling her to tell him more.

'I was curious,' she muttered. 'Okay, maybe I was jealous.' She shook her head, her mortification evident. 'You never even looked at me.'

'Of course I didn't.' He was shocked into speaking frankly. 'You were a child who hid in the kitchen all the time. I hardly saw you. And, yes, I was having a good time with other distractions. I needed those distractions then.'

'Because of your father and Naomi?'

Her soft question pierced his cool armour.

'I hated her.'

He was so shocked by Katie's confession, by the tired confusion in his head, that the truth washed out of him. His father's new wife had made them leave the home he loved and then...

'She took everything from me. She made him—' He broke off and strove for simplicity. 'He died and I blamed her. I still do.'

His father's heart had already been broken, but Naomi had delivered the fatal blow.

He glared at Katie, angered at what she'd made him reveal, but somehow unable to stop more words tumbling out. 'I was *alone*. It felt good. I'm not going to apologise for that.'

It hurt enough to admit even this. The truth was he'd been miserable. Bereft and grieving. And at the time he hadn't handled what was happening. The welcome of those lovers had been a brief respite from the bruising reality of his world being ripped apart.

'I was...'

'Seeking solace?' Katie finished his sentence softly.

He stilled. Solace? No. Not solace. That sounded too romantic, too refined. It attached too much meaning to what had been...

'No, it was just an escape,' he corrected her, blinding himself to the welts on his heart as he spoke. 'Sex feels good.'

'It's always just physical?' She frowned. 'Orgasms for everyone?'

He stiffened. 'Everyone loves a good orgasm, Katie, even you.'

'So there isn't an emotional connection?'

Her query caused him discomfort... He wasn't a user. He was a giver, right?

'I always ensure my partner has a good time,' he said, avoiding answering the actual question.

But she'd got what she wanted anyway. She'd exposed his shallow soul and he was angry with her. Because maybe it *wasn't* about all those women he'd been with at that time. Maybe he had just been seeking a fix—as temporary as it had been. Maybe he hadn't wanted to confront the hurt he'd been hiding from. He still didn't.

Yet even as he justified and deflected he felt flawed. Flayed. And he didn't like what she'd found in him.

'Yes,' Katie said, her face falling. 'I get that now.'

That was a knowledge she had because of *him*.

The thought of her enjoying escapist sex with some other guy skyrocketed his blood pressure.

'Damn it, Katie.' He frowned and sighed heavily.

'Maybe I *was* naive and judgey before.' She clutched her cup closer to her chest. 'But I'm right about stopping this now. You know I'm right.'

Yeah, as much as he hated the idea, he agreed with her. And he could hardly argue with her when he was the one who'd told her to speak up for what she wanted.

'Okay.' He nodded. 'No problem. I can handle a woman saying no to me.'

'Really?' As she turned he glimpsed something sharp in her eyes. 'That's not a challenge? Isn't it always a game to you?'

'It was when you were lying to yourself about how much you wanted me,' he said roughly, resenting the way she was challenging him now.

'You wanted me only to prove how much I wanted *you*?'

'No.'

At that first meeting in his office she'd hit his pride and he'd wanted to bite back. He'd told himself he'd get her to say yes for sport. But the truth was that real desire had taken hold in seconds. And now there could be nothing but blunt honesty.

'I just wanted you.'

He still did. But he didn't want to admit how different last night had felt. Not to her, and not to himself.

It was only because these were unusual circumstances. He'd never brought a woman to his island—that was what had made last night unique. There wasn't anything actually meaningful or special between them.

She stared at him for a moment. 'I'm sorry.' Worry straightened her soft mouth.

He realised she had actually been afraid of his reaction—of telling him what she wanted, denying him.

He pulled his head together and sent her a genuine smile, wanting her to relax. 'I can handle rejection, Katie. I'm not going to ask you to leave or end our arrangement just because you've had enough. You're allowed autonomy over your own damn body. Always.'

But she'd left an ache in his. And it was not unquenched lust. This was a loss that went deeper than that. In only a couple of soft-spoken sentences she'd stripped him of something he'd never realised he had but that he'd held dear.

His self-delusion.

Katie pulled on her bikini, bypassed the pool, and headed to the small beach she'd seen from the helicopter. She'd avoid Alessandro by exploring the island.

For almost an hour she walked along the waterline, paddling her feet and contemplating his reaction. But then she heard the chug of an engine growing louder. She paused halfway along the beach and watched the sleek little motorboat slowly come closer. Judging by the gleaming boat and its occupants' glamorous attire, she guessed they were friends of Alessandro's. And they'd clearly had this destination in mind.

'Ciao, bella!' the man called, a wide smile on his face as they came close to the shore.

'I'm not Bella,' she replied coolly.

The man wasn't put off—in fact he laughed. 'So it's true, Alessandro!'

She turned swiftly. Her husband was standing at the top of the beach behind her, wearing nothing but swim shorts. Katie swiftly suppressed her gasp of surprise that her spirits soared just at the sight of him. She blinked and tried not to stare like some lust-crazed nympho at all his bare skin. Acrid, smoky regret curled in her.

'What are you doing here, Vassily?' Alessandro asked, walking to join her at the waterfront.

'Satisfying my curiosity. We're all agog at the events.' The man was unabashed by Alessandro's even cooler tone—clearly a good friend, then. 'Since when have you been caught?'

'I keep my most precious things private—you know that, Vassily.' Alessandro ignored the question.

An unspoken communication passed between the two men before Vassily turned a bright smile on her. 'Come out with us for a quick spin,' he invited wickedly.

'Say no, Katie.'

She glanced at Alessandro and saw an unreadable brilliance in his eyes. She knew his friend was trying to goad him in some way, and while she should probably side with him, she was curious to know more. The imp of defiance blossomed within her.

'I only want to interrogate you,' Vassily added with roguish charm.

And she only wanted to escape Alessandro.

Rebellious fire raced in her veins. 'I've never been on a boat like yours.'

'Alessandro!' Vassily was audibly shocked. 'Have you kept her imprisoned on this island?'

'Getting into that rust bucket would be beneath you,' Alessandro informed her dryly.

Katie met Alessandro's gaze and read the displeasure there. For a moment she wondered if he was going to grasp her by the hand and hold her to his side.

She turned back to Vassily and forced a light laugh. 'He wants me to say no, but I'm not going to.'

'Defiant *and* beautiful…' Vassily taunted Alessandro.

Alessandro stared at Katie for another moment, a hint of retribution in his eyes, and then he splashed into the water.

'Are you coming too?' Vassily groaned with disappointment. 'How am I to torture the truth from her?'

'You're not touching her.' Alessandro turned and held out his hand to help her into the boat.

'Possessive?' Vassily commented dryly.

'Of my wife—yes.'

Katie couldn't look at either man as Alessandro helped her into the boat. He was only playing up his 'possessiveness' in front of his friends. She quickly sat and pasted on a smile for the woman who'd been watching the proceedings from behind her glamorous sunglasses.

Alessandro climbed aboard and shot Vassily a lazy look. 'Once around the island. Thirty minutes. That's all.' He leaned forward. 'Katie, this is Nina and Vassily. Both of them are untrustworthy annoyances.'

From his tone she knew he was teasing. Nina just had to be a model. She had gleaming black hair to her hips, smoky eyes, and a white string bikini that showed off every inch of her stunning physique.

'Would you like a drink?' Vassily offered with a laugh. 'There's champagne in the picnic basket.'

'No, thanks, it's a little early for me.'

So this was his world. Katie listened to their glib repartee, noting their insouciance and glamour. These were wealthy people avoiding boredom with their fast boats, fast women and party lifestyle.

She saw the glance Nina shot Alessandro, heard her low, laughing whisper, and stiffened. In a few months' time he'd be free to follow up that invitation if he wanted. She knew he wouldn't now, though. He'd made a promise to her in Vegas and for as long as they were married he'd keep it. But even so jealousy twisted. It was stupid of her when *she'd* said no to him. *She'd* stopped it.

Only three hours in and she regretted that rash decision.

Don't think about it.

'Do you stay here with Alessandro often?' she asked,

thinking she'd distract herself by getting what information she could from Vassily.

'No one gets to go on Alessandro's island—it's sacrosanct.'

'He doesn't lease it out when he's not here?' She frowned lightly.

'Oh, I wish! We'd all lease it year-round.'

Why had he told her he leased it out when he didn't? Why lie? And it didn't make sense. Alessandro was too astute a businessman to leave an asset like this unoccupied and not making him money. Moreover, he was known for his rapid turnaround of businesses. He flicked them on at a profit and moved to the next. Why hadn't he sold this place?

Well, actually, that she could understand—no one in their right mind would ever sell this slice of heaven.

She masked her frown with a smile as they circled around the island and sped past the high cliffs. They'd circled around half the island already.

Another small cove came into view. 'That beach is amazing.'

Vassily glanced at her and turned to Alessandro with surprise. 'You've not taken her swimming here?'

'We've been busy with other things.' Alessandro ran his fingertip across her bare shoulders. 'The sun is hot. We should get you back.'

'You've brought out his protective instincts,' Vassily said in apparent amazement. 'I never knew he had any.'

Katie turned back to the beach.

'A blushing bride, Alessandro?' Vassily positively marvelled. 'I'd never have thought.'

'You don't often think,' Alessandro retorted mildly. 'Take us home.'

'You can always come and stay with me if he gets too grumpy,' Vassily whispered to her as they returned to the main beach and he pulled the boat back into the shallows.

'I never get grumpy, Vassily. Unless someone tries to mess with what's mine.'

It was a barely veiled threat, playing up to his protective, possessive image. After all, for him it was always a game.

'I want to be alone with my wife—does that really surprise you?'

'No. And I don't blame you for keeping her your secret captive, Alessandro.' Vassily smirked. 'I'm only sorry you met her first.'

Katie breathed out in relief as she jumped back into the water and splashed to the relative safety of Alessandro's private beach. 'Bye, Vassily—bye, Nina.' She waved.

'Did you have fun?' Alessandro asked with an ironic inflection as they walked the path to the house.

'Your friends are nice.'

'They're too curious.'

'Because they care?'

He shook his head. Of course he'd deny any depth of emotion in any of his relationships.

'I bet you two make a fabulous duo. Two playboys on the prowl.' She grimaced.

'You're forgetting Nina,' he drawled.

She didn't want to think about Nina—it just made that stupid jealousy flare. 'I'm going to change,' she muttered.

'Wonderful.' With a vicious movement, he peeled off the path by the pool. 'I'm going to cool off.'

CHAPTER ELEVEN

KATIE SPENT THE night tossing and turning alone in her bed. She should have fallen asleep almost instantly, given she'd hardly had any sleep the night before. Instead she spent hours awake—burning up with restless regret.

They'd had a quiet dinner, talking about things that were not intimate, not important. He'd mentioned that the paperwork for White Oaks was well underway, and she'd be able to see it and sign it when they got back to London.

She'd spoken to Susan again, avoiding difficult questions by keeping the conversation about her foster mother's new carers. Susan seemed to enjoy their company. She sounded well cared for and happy—so Katie could relax a little, right?

Surely she'd made the right decision regarding Alessandro and her…? This feverish ache would soon ease. She'd lived without sensuality all her life—she'd get used to that again quickly, wouldn't she?

She rose early and opted to avoid both the pool and the beach, taking refuge in the garden, fossicking for fruit and herbs as she went. The plants were varied and verdant, and so diverse that she hurried back to the house to grab a basket to put her samples in.

Then she followed the crisscrossing paths through the formal gardens, eventually following one out into a forest-like area. She searched for wild herbs for a while, and then came upon another less-defined track. The small *Proprieta Privata* sign provoked her curiosity.

A few minutes along she saw a small cottage. It wasn't the quarters of the couple who lived on the island full-time—that was on the other side, nearer the new mansion. This small structure was clearly much older than any of the others, and it was tiny. As she paused to look at it the front door suddenly opened—and Alessandro walked out, an open book in his hand.

As he saw her a look of genuine shock flashed on his face. He was quick to recover, but his smile didn't quite smother the unguarded sadness in his eyes.

'I'm so sorry,' she said hurriedly, and backed up a step, realising she'd come upon him at a private moment. 'I didn't mean to intrude. I was just...'

'Avoiding me the same way I was avoiding you.'

She smiled ruefully. 'I've interrupted your reading. I'll go.'

'No, I wasn't even seeing the words.'

Embarrassed, she didn't know what to say.

He seemed to gather himself and glanced at the basket she was carrying. 'You've been busy.'

'Oh, yes.' She glanced down and belatedly realised just how much produce she'd picked. 'I hope you don't mind?'

'Why would I mind?' he growled. 'I like it when you speak your mind, Katie. I like it when you do what you want. You don't have to fit in to my schedule—you should feel free to do whatever you want here. I'm not going to send you away. Not because you don't want to sleep with me, or do whatever I want. I'm not like your foster father. You don't have to fall in line. You're safe. Nothing you could do would make me force you to leave. Just be *you*.'

She blinked, then smiled, surprised and touched by his mini-rant. She wished she could slide back into that teasing banter that she enjoyed so much.

'*Nothing* I could do?'

'I'm your husband—not your boss, your gaoler. Not any kind of authority. You don't have to ask my permission to do anything,' he added gruffly. 'Just do whatever you want.'

'Okay,' she agreed quietly.

He knew, didn't he? That all her life she'd had to seek permission, and that too many times she'd been scared to answer back when she'd wanted to. Maybe she ought to be embarrassed that he knew how weak she was... only he didn't seem to think she was, exactly...

He tossed the book down on an old wicker chair that stood near the cottage doorway and walked over to pick through the herbs in the basket. 'How do you know which ones aren't poisonous?'

'I don't know if you've heard of this thing called the internet...?

He chuckled and lifted one of the leaves to sniff it, that smile lingering in his eyes. 'My father would wander around with bunches of herbs, or some weird vegetable he'd picked from this garden.'

'You know, he was the one who taught me how to forage in the first place.'

Alessandro cocked his head, his eyes widening in surprise. 'My father did?'

'Those couple of summers he had at White Oaks, before he died.'

'You were just a kid.'

'That didn't mean everyone had to ignore me.' She shot him a sharp smile. 'He found me in the gardens when I was hiding from Brian's wrath one day… I think he took pity on me. He showed me some herbs and taught me various combinations.'

'He understood your interest?'

'He ignited it. He was an amazing man. Full of vitality and so generous.'

Alessandro scooped up the old hardback book he'd tossed down and gestured for her to sit. 'I had no idea he talked with you—but of course he would have.'

'He was nice to everyone. Socially gifted—like you.' She watched as he leaned against the old wall beside her.

He stared into space, seemingly lost in thought for a long moment. 'This was my parents' home.'

She was confused. 'The island?'

'This very cottage. We holidayed here when I was little. All our summers. Weekends.'

Really? No wonder the place was so special to him.

She sat very still, not wanting to interrupt him, hoping he'd tell her something more.

'After my mother died…my father didn't want to come back here.' He sighed. 'And then he and Naomi grew closer. She'd been working at the company for a while, establishing the London office. He brought her here, but she didn't like it.'

Katie's eyebrows lifted. How could anyone not like it here?

'There were too many memories of my mother.' He answered her unasked question with a pained smile.

'This is where Mamma convalesced when she was ill. Cancer. The hospital across the water is where she died. Naomi convinced him to sell the island just before they got married.'

Katie couldn't hold back. 'I can't believe Naomi wanted to get rid of this island.'

'She wanted everything *new*. She wanted him to live in England. New house. New life. More money. More success. Nothing of my mother or his heritage and their past. She wanted that wiped out. I think she was jealous of her. And I think Naomi's request broke his heart all over again.'

Alessandro gazed towards the cottage.

'It was the one thing I wanted,' he said. 'It took me years to get it back. The things are gone but the memories are here.'

She realised now that this place meant everything to him—more than his companies. More than anything. This was the one thing he'd chased and held on to.

'My father had plans for the big house, but Mamma always loved the cottage. This was where she liked to sit in the sun and read when she was too tired to do anything else.'

Katie waited, then looked at the stunning view over the waters to the mainland beyond and not into Alessandro's face as she finally asked a question and crossed her fingers that he'd answer.

'She was sick for a while?'

'Years,' he said flatly. 'It was hard on my father. He was managing the restaurants, expanding the food production. He wanted to make it a success and he nursed her at the same time. He'd come home late from the restaurants and do all his testing during the day, in the kitchen here. She'd sample everything for him.'

Katie smiled softly. 'What about you?'

'I'd try them too.' He half smiled.

That wasn't what she'd meant, and he knew it. But he'd deflected her away from himself—something she realised he often did with humour. And now she knew he'd been here all through his mother's illness.

'You helped care for her?'

There was a long moment of silence.

'When Mamma died, he had a kind of greyness to him... He had a heart attack a couple of weeks later. A broken heart from which I don't think he ever truly recovered.'

Katie's heart ached—it must have been terrifying for Alessandro. After his mother's long illness, to have almost lost his father so soon?

'And then Naomi...?'

'She came out from the UK to help with the company. They got together so quickly. I think he was trying to bury his grief, to feel better. Naomi wanted him to take the headquarters to England and focus on building the market there. He married her, gave up the island, his home, and worked himself into the ground. He gave her everything until his heart couldn't give any more. Love literally killed him.'

'And hurt you too.' So deeply.

No wonder he sought solace in sex—even if he denied it, that was what he'd been doing. He'd been torn from his home because he had wanted to support his father, probably while still grieving his mother's death. Only then he'd lost him too. And then Naomi had cut him out from his father's company.

'I'm okay, Katie,' he said.

'Really? You watched your mother suffer for a long time…you looked after her with your father. That's why you know what Susan needs—why you're angry with Brian for not doing a decent job. You lost your mother, you lost this place, you lost him… Alessandro—'

'Are you feeling sorry for me Katie?'

He sent her a semblance of that old wicked smile. But it had changed. It no longer hid the other elements within him. The vulnerability.

'Because don't. You know my life is amazing—'

'I'm glad you have this place back now,' she interrupted him. 'Your parents would—'

'I know,' he said quietly. 'It's the one place I won't part with. Never.'

'No.'

His heart was here. Deeply hidden and huge.

'I guess you feel this way about White Oaks,' he said gruffly.

Not quite. When she thought of her home now it was tinged with sadness. She realised how suffocated she'd felt there.

'I feel that way about *Susan*,' she said. 'White Oaks is beautiful, but it's also been a prison—like you said. Full of rules. And I was always afraid I was going to get sent away.'

She understood why Alessandro had helped her now. Because he understood so much more than she'd realised. He presented this carefree playboy façade, but beneath that was a hurt guy who'd lost everything that mattered to him most.

'What are you going to make with all that stuff?' he asked, pointedly looking back into the basket.

'I'm not sure.'

'Well, you've got to do *something* with it. It can't all go to waste now you've picked it.'

'Okay, I accept the challenge.'

Slowly they walked back along the path to the main house together and she desperately tried not to think about touching him. But she ached to hold him again.

'I thought you said you leased out the island, but Vassily told me you don't.'

Alessandro laughed, and cursed beneath his breath. 'In the early years I did, to help make it pay. I don't have to do that any more. I didn't *quite* lie to you.'

'No, you just didn't want to tell me how important it is to you.'

He paused and looked at her.

She turned to face him. 'Is it so hard admitting how much things might mean, Alessandro?'

The tension swelled between them again and he sent her a long, considering look. Then his gaze dropped to her basket.

'Go and concentrate your dangerous thinking on the contents of that basket, Katie. I think we might both prefer the results of that.'

She actually did as he'd suggested. Working in the kitchen had always been a kind of therapy for her—a displacement activity, a distraction from difficulties.

She lost track of time as she toyed with the assortment she'd gathered, trialling different herbs both in baking and in making something decent for dinner. But she couldn't quite shake her sadness for what he'd lost.

'You don't want a rest?'

She looked up as he walked back in, his face one big frown.

'It's been *hours*,' he added.

'It's been a good distraction,' she said with a rueful smile. 'It always is. Work is for you too, right?'

'Stop thinking you need to figure me out, Katie. I'm not that complicated. Work hard, play hard—every bit the cliché you said.'

'Really?' She gestured to a tray of lemon curd tartlets and tried to make a joke. 'So, you want to sample my wares?'

There was a pregnant pause and she glanced back and caught his eye.

'You know I do,' he muttered ruefully.

She knew he'd bitten back worse banter. She shot a look at him and laughed.

For a moment he joined in, but his laugh soon ended on a rueful sigh. 'The trouble is I know how good they're going to be already. I think that once I start I'm not going to want to stop.'

He rubbed his hand through his hair and looked at her with that old, wicked amusement.

'That *is* a problem,' she agreed with a light laugh.

He bit into one anyway, and closed his eyes briefly before nodding. 'Yeah, I knew it. These are even better than that sauce the other day. You're very talented, *dolcezza*.'

'No—'

'Take the compliment.'

She fell silent, pressing down on her smile.

'You tried to tell me it's all about those heritage fruit trees. It isn't, Katie. You're not reliant on the orchards at White Oaks. You can make amazing creations no matter where the ingredients come from. Have more faith in yourself. Your stuff is good because it's *yours*. Trust your taste. Your judgement. Make other things yours too.' He leaned over the bench, energy suddenly radiating from him. 'You know, I could launch a bid for Zetticci Foods...'

She stared at him in amazement.

'A hostile take-over. They're in a bad way. With you at the helm we could turn it around.'

She gaped for another second, then laughed. 'You're kidding?'

'Maybe it's time for Naomi to retire.' His energy somehow seemed to increase. 'You make a premium product, Katie. You could make a huge success of it.'

'You're crazy.'

'You just made me the most delicious thing I've eaten using little more than a few leaves from the garden. You know taste. Flavour. I believe in you, Katie. You should believe in you too.'

'I couldn't run a whole massive company.'

'I'd put in a management team to support you.'

She couldn't take her gaze off the fire in his. 'You want the company back? The way you have your home here back?'

'Actually, no.' He shook his head. 'It's only one option for you. You could expand White Oaks if you don't want to take on Zetticci. Or you could start something completely new. Whatever you choose, you need to make the most of your gift. You need to do something, *dolcezza*, you're too talented to go to waste. And I can help you.'

He truly meant it and she was truly touched. The fact that he believed in her gave her a lift that no one had ever given her.

But she knew what would happen. As soon as she was established and the company was viable he'd get bored. He'd sell and move on... He was always able to walk away because he never became emotionally involved in anything. He'd locked what heart he had into this place—where his history was.

'All of those options would take months, maybe years, to really become something,' she said. 'You don't want to be tied to me for that long,' she added bravely. 'We shouldn't complicate this even more.'

'I'm good at separating my business life from my personal life, Katie.'

He didn't have a personal life. At least, not a meaningful one.

'Yeah? Well, I can't compartmentalise as well as you can.' She paused. 'I appreciate your support, but I'm not going to be your latest business project. You've done enough for me.'

He watched her for another moment, then seemed to withdraw. 'Okay. Then we should go back to London. Check on Susan…face Brian. I don't think there's any point delaying any longer.'

She maintained her slight smile with all the control she could muster, but she'd frozen inside.

'It will remove us from temptation too.' A lopsided smile didn't quite reach his eyes. 'We'll figure out our living arrangements. I travel a lot. You won't have to see me all that often. I just ask that you stay at my place through the week. Weekends with Susan. Something like that?'

'Of course,' she readily agreed. 'Anything.'

He shot her a look and they both laughed, that newly forming ice thawing a fraction.

She only just bit back the apology she knew he'd hate to hear. Smiling, she looked up into his face. For a moment they faced each other, frozen for a beat of time.

She just knew he was thinking about kissing her. For a moment she wanted him to. He would be so easy to have an affair with, but even easier to fall in love with.

But that was the last thing he wanted, and she thought she understood why a little now.

'Old habits are very easy to fall into,' he said softly.

'And very hard to break.' She nodded.

She made herself look away from him. He was too handsome, too tempting. Smart, funny, loyal, kind… but emotionally contained.

He wasn't the wild playboy she'd once thought he was. He was private and hurt. And actually as isolated and as alone as she.

CHAPTER TWELVE

ALESSANDRO DRUMMED HIS fingers on the steering wheel, releasing the tension building within. He was so aware of her emotions he seemed to be absorbing them. She seemed unnervingly attuned to his moods too. As he'd told Vassily the other day, he kept the things most precious to him private, yet somehow he'd ended up spilling half his life story to her back in Italy. And as she'd listened the soft compassion in her clear eyes had made him speak even more.

Now yet more memories stirred as they drove through the village near White Oaks. Memories long-buried that impacted his usual carefree demeanour. Usually nothing meant enough for him to get that upset about it. It made making deals easier when he could be clinical. He'd be clinical about this too—somehow.

'The village seems smaller,' he commented, to slice through the strained atmosphere.

The energy in the car crackled.

'I'm sorry I've made you come back,' she said suddenly in a small voice.

He hated hearing that apology—the anxiety that simmered beneath her beauty. But he knew he wasn't really the source of her upset. She was worried about Susan. And scared to see Brian.

He was compelled to reassure her with the reality. None of this was her fault. He smiled at her. 'I'm the one driving—you haven't dragged me here.'

She didn't smile back. 'They kicked you out when you'd already lost so much. They took Aldo's company.' She dragged in a breath. 'You must hate the place—and I've made you *buy* it.'

'I could have said no,' he pointed out simply. 'Stop worrying about me. All that was a long time ago. Zetticci was Dad's. I know who I am. I know what I've done since.' He reached out and squeezed her hand. 'Don't feel bad for me, Katie. I know you've spent all your life caring for Susan and being careful around Brian. You don't need to do either of those things with me.'

Beneath his hand hers tensed, and he saw her blink a couple of times.

'I think I should still care about how you're feeling,' she said huskily.

A ball of discomfort tightened low in his gut. She was so disarmingly honest sometimes. He turned back to focus on driving instead of staring at her.

He cleared his throat as he turned down the long driveway of the estate. 'The gardens look even more magnificent than I remember.'

'Susan might be in a wheelchair now, but she still supervises the plantings like an army general.' She looked at the trees and exhaled shakily. 'I can't wait to see her.'

But when he pulled up outside the main house Katie didn't undo her seat belt, or make any attempt to move.

'You're worried about seeing him?' he prompted.

She swallowed and nodded.

Alessandro unclipped his belt and leaned across so that he could look into her pretty eyes properly. 'You have no trouble standing up to me,' he murmured lightly. 'I'm a brilliant businessman, but you negotiated with me and won. You have me wrapped around your little finger and saying yes to your every request.'

A small smile slowly curved her lips.

'You've put me in my place with no problem at all,' he reminded her with a little wink. 'Besides, what can he do to you now?'

Katie squared her shoulders and knocked on the door. Alessandro was right. She could handle Brian—and more importantly she was going to see Susan.

To her surprise, Brian was smiling as he opened the door and welcomed them into the wide foyer. He was also alone.

'Where's Susan?' Katie frowned as she looked around for signs of her foster mother.

Brian ignored her question. 'It's been a long time, Alessandro.'

'Where's Susan, Brian?' Katie asked again.

'She'll be here shortly.'

Brian's smile seemed superglued on, and he still hadn't so much as looked at Katie.

'I thought we should have a minute to fully settle the situation first.'

'The situation is settled,' she said crisply. 'We're only here to see Susan.'

He finally faced her. His swift glance took in her new clothes and that horrible crocodile smile widened more. 'I underestimated you, Katie. Alessandro's backing is even more secure than Carl's would have been. We can restore White Oaks completely. You won't have to spend hours making those silly sauces any more. All that effort for such little return.' He stepped closer. 'You've done well. Everybody wins.'

He was so dismissive, so ignorant, and he didn't even realise how cruel he was being. He had no idea how much her work meant to her.

'Seriously...?' Katie muttered with appalled amazement.

This was why he was smiling and not shouting at her for defying him? Because he thought she'd done a better deal than the craziness he'd arranged? And now he was acting welcoming in order to manipulate her, because it was in *his* best interests?

'Alessandro.' Brian turned back to her silent husband. 'Why don't we—?'

'Where's Susan, Brian?' Katie interrupted impatiently.

He shot her a displeased look.

She turned her back on him and walked into the hallway. 'She knew we were coming. I talked to her about it last night...' She trailed off and listened, but the house was eerily silent. She looked back at Brian.

He glared at her, and that old meanness tightened his features. 'I knew we had things to discuss privately, so I told her you'd changed the time you were arriving.'

'You...*what*?'

'She's out with one of her new companions. They're very thoughtful and caring, those nurses. Susan's happier than she's been in years.'

Katie brushed off that deliberate dig, still getting

her head around what he'd done. 'You lied to her about when I was coming?'

Her pulse roared in her ears. How typically controlling. He'd know how much Katie wanted to see Susan. This was a petty way of inflicting pain. But Susan had been looking forward to seeing Katie too.

'How could you do that to her?' Katie stared at him.

'She'll see you soon enough,' Brian shrugged.

Hurt exploded. 'The only reason we're here is to see *her*. I want to ensure Susan's happiness and security at White Oaks.'

'And apparently you've achieved that by marrying Alessandro. Well done.'

She gaped at him. 'All that matters to me is her happiness. You know, I have no idea why she stays married to you, but that's her choice. Here's *my* choice—you can live here, but only as long as you care for Susan properly. No more "conferences", Brian. No more gambling. If you put one foot out of line it's all over.'

He stepped closer. 'You can't tell me what to do.'

'The way you've told *me* what to do all my life?' She'd laugh if she didn't feel so bitter. 'You don't *have* to do as I say, but as I now own this property—'

'You manipulative little—'

'What?' she interrupted furiously. She wasn't going to let him berate her again. 'You never let me feel safe here—or like I belonged. You always threatened me to make me do what you wanted. No more, Brian. You can't bully me now.'

'Because you've brought *him* with you?' he sneered.

'Because I don't care any more,' she yelled. 'Because I'm doing what *I* want. What's best for me and what's best for Susan and that's it.' She drew breath and stared at the defiance in his eyes. 'She's not coming back for hours, is she?'

He didn't answer.

'Do anything like this again and you're gone.'

She turned on the spot and walked out of the house, instinctively turning towards the silent shaded safety of her youth—away from Brian, away from the conflict that had always festered…away from Alessandro. She didn't want him to *see*—

'Katie.'

He caught her shoulders as she stumbled. She bowed her head but didn't turn. She didn't want to look at him. She was too hurt.

All her life Brian had made her feel inadequate, as if she were a disappointment—only there on sufferance because Susan had wanted her. He'd controlled her with that sense of obligation—playing on her gratitude and guilt.

'You were amazing,' Alessandro muttered, pulling her back to rest against him.

'No…' She shook her head and resisted his embrace. 'No, I wasn't. I ran away.'

He turned her in his arms and searched her face, muttering something low and indecipherable, then pressed her head against his chest and cradled her. 'I'm sorry he hurt you,' he muttered gruffly into her hair.

She knew he saw her turmoil and sadness. Her hands reached out of their own accord, resting on his waist. His warmth and strength burned through his shirt. All she wanted was to feel better. To feel that someone wanted her. Her birth parents hadn't wanted her. Nor had Brian. And he'd kept her from seeing Susan today.

Susan who loved her but whom she was going to lose too soon…

Her heart tore. 'How can he still hurt me?' she whispered.

'Because you care,' Alessandro muttered against her hair. 'It's complicated. He raised you…part of you might always want his approval, might always love him. Even when he's let you down.'

Katie lifted her head and gazed into Alessandro's eyes. How was he so compassionate and insightful and complex…and so right? Was it because he knew something of how she felt?

'Did it feel as if your father had let you down when he married Naomi?'

He froze for a moment, but then nodded. 'I wanted him to be happy, but I couldn't understand how he could be happy with *her*…'

Katie smiled sadly. 'Was *any* woman going to live up to your mother?'

He sent her an equally sad smile and admitted it. 'Probably not. But he could have done better. He could have found someone kind. She wasn't. And he wasn't strong enough to move, to work all those hours… But he wanted to please her—he wanted to be loved.'

Katie's heart curled in. 'I can understand that,' she said softly. 'Most of us want to be loved.'

Alessandro shook his head. 'No. Some of us don't want that at all.' He smiled at her. 'Too much drama.'

She knew he was deliberately making a joke, but she couldn't smile back. 'Too much hurt?'

He paused. 'That too.'

The truth hovered between them—an invisible, impenetrable wall.

He pressed his palm to her cheek. 'Katie—'

She didn't want to talk any more. She didn't want to think any more.

'Don't be nice to me,' she whispered.

He could never give her what she really wanted but she didn't care about that. She just wanted to feel better.

'What should I be, then?' he asked with a remnant of that old teasing glint. 'All mean and horrible like him?' He cocked his head and the glint brightened into something fiercer and his smile faded. 'I don't care if that's what you're used to—you're not getting it from me.'

A fierce bubble of emotion fizzed in her chest. 'What *am* I getting, then?'

'What do you want?'

Pure emotion pulsed. Hurt, angry, aching for something, she gazed at him. 'Solace.'

His chest rose and fell, and she snatched a glimpse of turmoil reflected in his eyes. But then he bent and kissed her gently. Too gently.

'Why have you stopped?' That wasn't what she wanted.

With a rough groan he kissed her again—and the floodgates were opened.

Katie clung to him, pouring her need into his kiss. She lost everything in that one searing kiss—all reason, all hurt, even her footing. She was literally swept off her feet. But somehow he was with her, pressing so close on the warm summer grass. And there was nothing smooth or practised in this. It was simply a kiss—soul-deep, urgently seeking to satisfy a longing so intense neither could stop.

She shook, unwilling and unable to break the seal of their kiss. And he was too. As their mouths clung their hands moved the clothing necessary and suddenly he was there—*all* there—right where she was hot and wet and hungry and needing his fierce, hard strength.

She sobbed into his kiss as he gave her what she needed. Locked together, their connection was deep and intimate, and somehow their physical closeness became an exposition of something else altogether. A welter of emotions tossed within her—and warmth of a different kind radiated over the intense heat of pure passion.

But she couldn't stop to define it because she'd already exploded, her body radiating that desperate, devastating delight.

But even as she struggled to recover, struggled to stand and walk with him back to the car, she knew the difficult truth. It still wasn't enough.

'We'll come back soon. We won't tell him when. You'll see Susan, I promise.'

'I know.'

Alessandro glanced at her quickly, then turned back to the road. He was struggling not to speed, not to get them the hell out of there as fast as possible—away from what had just happened.

Not Brian and his petty meanness. But Katie and him.

He'd done the one thing she'd asked him not to. And while she'd been willing at the time that was only because she'd been emotional. Vulnerable.

His emotions churned—want, pain, denial. He'd wanted to reach out to her. He'd been desperate to see her smile again—to hold her close and comfort her. Yes, to offer solace.

But holding her close had led to other things. The need to connect with her had been primal and he'd done it the one way he knew best. Physically. He'd meant only a kiss, but passion had overtaken him. All he'd wanted was to heal the bruise on her heart, but what he'd done was put her at risk.

'I'm sorry,' he said tightly. 'I shouldn't have—'

'I wanted it too,' she interrupted quietly.

'No, I lost control. I didn't use anything' He'd had unprotected sex for the first time in his life. He'd never lost control like that before. 'You might—'

'I'm on birth control,' she said softly.

He was so stunned he almost slammed on the brakes. That flash of a future, that wisp of an image of Katie cradling their baby, wasn't the shocking possibility it had been a second ago.

'Since when? You were—'

'I'm on it for other reasons,' she mumbled. 'But it means that what just happened won't...'

'Have long-term consequences?' he finished for her.

But it felt like a lie. When he ought to feel instant relief, he felt a sinking inside instead. Surely not disappointment? What was wrong with him?

That hadn't been escape he'd sought to offer her. It hadn't been solace. Hadn't he taken advantage because it had eased his *own* demons to hold her? Because he'd been desperate to touch her? He'd ached for her softness, her surrender.

He'd hated the exclusion and isolation from her in these past days. He'd hated the restrictions she'd put on them. He'd assumed his fascination with her would fade, whether they burned out their desire or not. He'd thought that if it were starved it would die. It hadn't. And even sated again it still hadn't.

Could he really blame this on old habits? The other

day he'd recoiled from her suggestion that there was something emotionally needy in his liaisons. But wasn't it exactly that? Yes, he used sex as an escape—for fun, to alleviate boredom or stress…but he also used it to hide from his hurts.

The trouble was that now he'd recognised that those hurts were still there… But, even so, what he'd done with Katie hadn't just been about using sex to assuage their pain. It hadn't been just rampant libido either. Those weak justifications minimised what had happened.

The truth was that too-quick moment under the trees had been the most intimate experience of his life. Never had he wanted to feel as close to someone, to give to someone. And in the aftermath he ached.

Grimly he parked the car in the basement garage of his London apartment and escorted her into the elevator. He'd have to remove himself—temporarily shift into another apartment. He walked through the lounge, tossing the keys on the table as he went. He'd call the building manager and see if there was a unit free.

'Alessandro.'

Reluctantly he glanced at her. She stood in the middle of his lounge. Her face was pale and tear-stained and her pretty dress was crumpled. She'd never looked as beautiful. If he was going to leave, it had to be now.

'I'm taking you to bed, Alessandro,' she said, with that quiet boldness he loved to see in her.

'Are you?' He swallowed and felt his self-control slip. He tried to joke. 'I thought you didn't want to make things any more complicated?'

'I think it's a little late for that.'

'No, it's not.' It couldn't be.

'You like control. Are you afraid that if you give too much away you'll lose control altogether?'

'Katie—'

'I'm not going to hurt you.' She stepped towards him.

As if *that* was the issue! 'You're no longer afraid that I might hurt you?' he growled.

She shrugged carelessly. 'I want that escape. Just for a while.'

'Is that really all it is, *dolcezza*?' It didn't feel like it to him any more—and suddenly he was angry. 'It's always been an escape for me,' he said harshly. 'It wasn't always about the woman I was with—more about the thrill of the chase, the orgasms.'

She flinched—then froze.

'I get off on seeing my partner get hers too. I always like doing that for her. But you…it's different.' Somehow it mattered more. 'I don't just get off from making you climax,' he muttered, almost malevolently. 'It's an imperative. I ache to taste you. To make you shake. To hear you scream. I want nothing more than to render you mindless…so that all you can do is beg for me. Because that's how much I want you. I don't get off from that. I live for it.'

He drew in a sharp breath, half appalled at what he'd just admitted. He watched as Katie's skin was burnished with the most beautiful blush.

But she brushed a lock of hair behind her ear and didn't take her shy but hungry eyes off him. 'So why are you all the way over there?'

Because he couldn't seem to move.

Because he couldn't quite process the depth of this.

She walked over until she was a mere breath away.

'What do you want?' she asked. 'You asked me to say what I wanted. Now I'm asking you.'

His tongue was tied.

Her expression softened. 'It's hard, isn't it?'

He swallowed. 'Harder than you'd believe,' he huffed in a lame quip.

'I'm not going to help you with that unless you speak up.' She smiled and leaned that little bit closer. 'It's only fair, Alessandro.'

She'd turned his own tease on him—except he didn't want it to be a tease any more. The threat of denial—of her leaving him aching—felt like a whip over his heart. He curled his hands into fists. It was too intense.

'Tell me what you want from me.'

He just wanted her. Not to forget, or escape, or soothe all his aches… He just wanted to hold her close. But it seemed he'd lost his words.

'I…'

'What?'

He could hardly think. He felt too hot, too broken. Her flecked eyes flashed with confusion, compassion, heat. He dropped his gaze and stared at her mouth because he couldn't continue to drown in her eyes.

'You want me to kiss you?' she breathed. 'Where?'

He didn't care. Anywhere. He just needed her touch. *'Accarezzami…'*

She understood. She was there already. Sensations swept over him as her hands caressed him and she kissed him with her soft, sweet mouth. For one last second he stayed still, trying to hold it all back. But then it was too late.

Almost savagely he scooped her into his arms and stormed towards his bedroom to have it all.

CHAPTER THIRTEEN

KATIE DIDN'T JUST say yes. She demanded more. And he didn't let her down. He sent her into a world she'd known existed but had never dreamed she'd step into. A world of freedom and choice.

Each morning Alessandro took her to a different market—they'd scoped them out together online, part of the research he reckoned she needed to do. Laughing, but loving it, she chose ingredients, tools.

On their return to the apartment he'd shut himself in his study to work while she tested her new finds in the kitchen. A few hours later he'd emerge and taste what she'd been working on.

By then their sensual tension was too fraught to ignore. Beneath his ministrations Katie had unleashed a hidden, long-denied side of herself—the demanding side. And she had more than accepted it—she indulged it. Again and again.

Alessandro was intense, passionate and insatiable. And he held nothing back from her now. It was so intense, so physical…it was almost frantic. And it always felt fantastic.

He refused to let her cook dinner. Instead they worked their way around the finest restaurants in the city. More market research, according to Alessandro. Sometimes then they went straight home. Sometimes they went to the gilt champagne bar half a block from his apartment and met up with Vassily and Nina and a few other of his friends. It turned out that Nina owned a leisurewear company. And now Katie had pushed past her own insecurity she realised the glamorous woman was really nice—and helpful.

As the days passed she grew increasingly comfortable in her clothes, in her conversation, and with her lover. She even teased him as they talked. But the more she settled in to his lifestyle the edgier Alessandro seemed to become. More attentive. More protective. Almost *possessive*.

'You guys should still be in Italy on honeymoon,' Nina teased her suddenly as they sat together in the bar one evening.

Katie looked at her in surprise.

'I just intercepted that look Alessandro sent you from across the room and you should definitely still be on that island, away from everybody else.' Nina laughed. 'Uh-oh, he's headed this way and looking at you like you're some tasty morsel he's going to swallow in one mouthful.'

Katie glanced over and her gaze instantly collided with his. Electricity arced—and it wasn't his dangerously handsome good-looks, it was the intensity in his whole demeanour, that aura of something unleashed. Tingling awareness shot to her toes as he strode over and held out his hand.

'Bye, Nina.' Katie shot the woman an embarrassed smile as she laced her fingers through Alessandro's and left with him.

'Is something wrong?' she asked him once they were out on the pavement.

Waves of emotion rippled from him. 'You can't look at me like that and not expect me to react,' he muttered.

'You were looking at *me* like that!' she laughed.

He smiled, but she still sensed tension within him. Ripples of sensuality swept through her as they walked.

'I was jealous,' he said gruffly.

'I was talking to *Nina*!' Katie laughed again.

'Nina enjoys the company of attractive people, male or female. She's fascinated by both...'

Katie laughed again, hugely amused. 'Well, Nina is not fascinated by me. We were talking about running a business. She has a lot of experience. I can learn from her.'

'You can learn from *me*,' he pointed out with roguish arrogance as he held the apartment door for her. 'I too have a lot of experience.'

'As a woman in enterprise?'

He chuckled, but then his sensuality simmered over again. 'I don't like it when other people look at you. When other people interest you. When other people make you laugh,' he said, pure seduction. 'You're *my* wife.'

'So only *you* can advise me? Only *you* can make me laugh?' she teased, placing her palm against his roughened jaw.

'No. But only I can do this.'

He pulled her closer and kissed her.

It was no longer solace, no longer an escape. It was all ecstasy.

Katie closed her eyes and drowned in desire, denying the edge of desperation still sharpening within...

* * *

He should have known she'd surprise him. In the last week she'd blossomed. She held her own with the likes of Vassily and Nina and his other friends. She saw through their banter for what it was and threw equally teasing barbs and brilliant smiles. She'd come alive as they explored the city, trialling all kinds of creations in the kitchen...

Yet why should any of that be a surprise? She'd made a success of her sauces. She'd made those recipes. She'd picked the fruit, sold to customers. She was outstandingly capable. Just because she'd barely travelled more than twenty-miles from White Oaks, it didn't mean she was going to be shy and socially inept.

She just hadn't had the chance before. And now she was taking to it like a duck to water.

Yet he still felt oddly protective of her, knowing that she'd do anything for those she barely knew and everything for those she loved. Knowing that, though her smile came more readily, that rosy flush still swarmed over her skin at his touch.

She was a sweet woman who burned hotter than any other and he didn't want her to change. But she hadn't. She wasn't. She'd just become more herself. She shone—beautiful, proud, confident. Part of him enjoyed the way she glittered when they were out together, and yet part of him wished he'd kept her hidden, so she was all just his.

But that wouldn't have been fair. She'd been hidden most of her life. Kept on that old estate, starved of true freedom by a foster father determined to control her. And Alessandro couldn't keep her for ever—life didn't work like that.

The next night Katie spoke at length to Nina again. Alessandro watched from a distance, knowing she was aware of his scrutiny. She smouldered at him from across the room. He let her tease him until he had to hustle her out before he lost control altogether.

He saw Vassily's arched eyebrow as he whisked her away. He didn't damn well care.

He kissed her as they were driven back to his penthouse. He didn't make it to the bedroom—pulling her to the floor to satisfy the searing lust that overcame him. Her enthusiasm for life literally had him on his knees.

She laughed, and her emerging playfulness arrested his heart. So he worked until she screamed. And then he carried her to his bed and did it all again, until she sighed and drifted off in sated, exhausted slumber.

But he couldn't sleep. He couldn't shake the sensation of impending loss. It knocked against his ribcage, trying to break in and hit the block inside that was his heart. He wasn't going to let it in.

Hours later, he was still awake. Still bothered by a worry he couldn't define, still feeling uneasy at the intensity with which he needed to be with Katie.

Maybe he needed to restore his usual routine—he couldn't ignore the rest of his life for ever. Katie seemed settled, happy, they were managing the moment just fine... Things could return to normal, right?

'I need to go into the office. I've avoided it too long.' Alessandro walked into the kitchen early, looking far too fine in his navy suit and tie.

'Sure thing.' Katie masked her disappointment with a smile. 'I promise not to burn the place down while you're gone.'

'Great. Then I'll see you later.'

She couldn't quite look at him as he left, and their goodbye was too awkward. They weren't anything like a normal newly married couple.

She worked in the kitchen for a while as a distraction. It wasn't quite enough, so she phoned Susan as well.

'Lemon filling today,' she said, and smiled as she held the phone under chin and stirred the mixture at the same time. 'I think it's pretty good. I'll bring some to you in a few days.'

'You'll be able to see the Madame Hardy rose that's just bloomed.'

'The white one?' Katie had her head around all the herbs, but the roses not so much. And in this old familiar chat her heart ached. She missed her foster mother. 'I can come and see you today, if you like. The train wouldn't take—'

'No, darling,' her foster mother said softly. 'You should be with your husband.'

Should she?

She knew her foster mother was as old-fashioned as the roses she grew, but Katie couldn't understand how Susan could accept Brian's controlling behaviour. How could she not see his lack of kindness? Katie wasn't as forgiving. She wasn't as accepting of...*less*.

Alessandro's image flickered in her mind. She pushed down the wave of discomfort. What they were doing wasn't *less*, wasn't it?

Distractedly she ended the call to Susan, then walked through the apartment. She wished he hadn't gone to work—she missed him a stupid amount already and he'd only been gone a few hours.

She tiptoed to his study, unable to resist her curiosity. It wasn't as neat as she'd expected. Various folders were scattered over a table in the centre of the room. She recognised the names on some of them—buildings he owned, mostly. But then she spotted one with her name on the front. It was set to the side of the others and not hidden at all. A sticky note on the top had a reminder written on it: *Get Katie to sign.*

Her heart skipped a beat, then sped up. In Italy he'd said the White Oaks paperwork would be ready for her when they returned to England. She opened the cover and blinked at the number of pages inside. It wasn't just the documents about his purchase of White Oaks. There was more—about them.

Three pages detailed all the options for declaring their marriage voidable if they wanted to seek an annulment. She glanced at the date at the bottom. It had been written the morning after their marriage. There was also a draft divorce agreement. She blinked at all the zeroes on the pay-out figure she was to receive on settlement. Cold sweat filmed her forehead. The inevitable end of their marriage was presented here with perfect clarity, in simple black and white.

Why had he wanted to do all this so soon after that hideous wedding? Why was he being so financially generous upon her release?

Because he wanted to be free and he'd needed to know the best way to proceed.

He'd never intended on going through with their marriage of convenience in the beginning. He'd only strung her along to get her far enough away from Brian for her to be able to think clearly. He'd openly admitted that. Only then they'd had that message about the engagement announcement and she'd got scared. And he'd whisked her up the aisle to stop her breaking down.

He'd given in.

He'd even given her the sex she'd wanted. He'd known she'd wanted that right from the start. No doubt an experienced man like Alessandro always knew. Besides, women always wanted sex from him.

She'd been so naive. She was his pity project—his Cinderella. He'd dressed her up, he'd taken her to parties, he'd even helped develop possibilities for her own company, had believed in her skill... He'd been soothing over all her insecurities because beneath that arrogant playboy persona he was actually a nice guy. And of *course* he had to protect his company, his own interests, his *name*. He couldn't let this marriage fall apart too soon. He'd been keeping her happy.

But all the intimacy they'd shared was based on a sham. And it had always been going to end.

She stalked through the apartment, unable to release the frenetic energy that was coiling tightly within her. She needed to take action. She'd thought she'd escaped the restrictions of her old life, but in reality she'd ceded control of everything to Alessandro the second she'd sought him out. While he'd done all she'd asked, and then some, he'd always had his exit plan, and he'd want her to sign on the dotted line eventually.

She needed to reclaim not just her own future but her own *now*.

She ought to feel free. White Oaks was secure, Susan was happy and cared for, and she'd silenced Brian and knew she could now ignore him. She had everything, right?

No. Now she knew what she really wanted. A real

NATALIE ANDERSON   191

relationship. She didn't want to be with a man she'd bargained into marrying her. She wanted to be with someone who actually wanted her—only her—for *her*. That wasn't Alessandro. He didn't love her. She wasn't what he wanted, and she wasn't enough for him. She'd known that from the start, but somehow she'd forgotten for a while—he was so seductive, so good at making *her* feel good.

This reminder of reality hurt.

She dragged in a shivering breath. It hurt a lot.

She'd been the one to initiate that kiss in the orchard. Alessandro probably hadn't wanted to reject her at that moment because she'd already been crying. She'd even asked him for it—for escape, for solace. He hadn't said no because he was too *kind*.

And she'd asked again back at his apartment. In fact, she'd demanded. Again he'd said yes. For a moment she'd felt all that warmth and intimacy and believed in unions and love. But that didn't mean he cared for her in any great way. No more than he cared for any other woman who'd been in his life.

The guy adored sex. He was the first to admit that. It wasn't an expression of *love*, it was physical pleasure— escape and release. Even when he'd said it was different with her, he'd still meant it was only physical. Her instincts after their first time together had been right. She'd known it would mean more to her.

Anger shot through her. Why didn't she ever get it all? Why was she never enough?

She'd not been wanted by her birth family. Not wanted by Brian. Not wanted enough by Susan for her to really fight for her...

And Alessandro would want someone else very soon.

He had no intention of this relationship lasting. He never had.

She'd been starved of attention for so much of her life she'd been willing to accept anything he cared to offer her. That made her more like Susan than she'd realised. But, worse than that, she'd been like Brian too—*using* Alessandro, taking advantage of his innate generosity.

The realisation hurt.

She had to deal with it. She couldn't maintain this facsimile of a marriage. Couldn't stick around waiting for him to get bored and pull out the divorce document. No more lies, no more pretence. There had to be nothing but honesty.

Three hours later she froze halfway down the hall as she heard the door unlock.

'Katie?' Alessandro paused just over the threshold, a wary expression stealing over his face as he studied her. 'What's with the scared rabbit look? Is everything okay?'

Nothing was okay.

'What's happened?' He closed the door behind him, his eyes narrowing on the overnight bag she'd placed by the entrance. 'Are you going somewhere?'

'I need to leave, Alessandro.'

'Leave? Why?' His expression sharpened. 'Is it Susan? You need me to take you to her?'

His concern shattered her. 'It's not that. I can't ever thank you enough for helping me with her. But you were right,' she said softly. 'I didn't need to get married to help her. I don't have to feel like I owe everyone everything. Not even you. I can just say no.'

'So you're saying no to me? To *us*? Just like that?'

He cleared his throat and walked towards her. 'You've just decided it's over?'

She held her hands together tightly. 'You asked your lawyer to check the validity of our marriage.'

He checked his pace and then breathed out. 'Is that what this is about? You looked at the paperwork?'

'There was a lot of it. You explored all the options.'

'Of course—that's what due diligence is. I thought you'd want to see it. I've never held anything back from you, *dolcezza*.'

'Haven't you?' She threw him a sceptical glance. 'You thought I'd want to see that amount in the divorce settlement? How much you're prepared to pay to be rid of me?'

'To be rid of you? Or to help you?' He stopped about three feet away from her, but he seemed to be looking right into her soul. 'In the eyes of the world, we're married.'

It was all about that façade... 'But it's not real.'

'Isn't it?' he asked sharply. 'Are we not living as a married couple? Aren't we intimate? Sharing?'

'*What* are we sharing?' she asked. 'I am *taking* what you are *giving*. And I'm saying you don't have to give any more.'

'I don't "have to give"?' He laughed that bitter laugh that sounded so wrong on him. 'I never "have" to do anything, Katie. I've wanted to do everything I've done with you.'

But he didn't want to give her what she really wanted. 'This was a mistake from the start.'

Seeing that report had been the catalyst to finally make her see sense. She'd used him too much for too long and in the process she'd lost her heart.

She whirled away from him, hurt and unable to hide it. 'I should have married Carl.'

Hard hands on her shoulders spun her around. 'Take that back.' He glared at her.

Somehow she was against the wall and she couldn't escape his fury.

'Take that back *now*,' he demanded roughly.

His anger astonished her. Worse was the familiar tug low in her belly. Would she always want him beyond reason? Beyond caring even for herself?

'You would have been miserable with him.' Alessandro's gaze drilled into her, daring her to deny it.

'I'm more miserable now.'

His eyes widened and he actually paled. 'You regret being with me that much?'

No. She didn't regret a second of it. How could she? When it had been the most intense, amazing, infuriating time of her life? But it mattered so much that it hurt to *breathe*. She'd always be on edge. Waiting. Knowing that soon enough he'd be bored and decide to initiate the divorce. And then he'd be gone. How could she put herself through that?

'I never would have slept with him,' she explained with pained honesty. 'Then this wouldn't have happened.'

'It's only because we've been sleeping together that things have become complicated?'

Her eyes filled with acidic tears. 'Of course not.'

It was because she'd fallen in love with him. And that was the last thing he'd want.

'You don't want to stay?' His bafflement hurt all the more.

She laughed weakly. She'd give almost anything to

stay. But she'd slowly shrivel up and die a slow painful death here. Because her heart would beat alone, ripped out to remain where it wasn't wanted, slowly bleeding out its last.

'For what?' she asked bitterly. 'You to finally get tired of me?'

He looked shocked. 'Katie—'

'Why does all this have to be on *your* timeline?' she exploded as she heard the denial in his voice. 'Why can it only be over when *you've* had enough?'

He brushed the backs of his fingers down her jawline. 'Have you really had enough, Katie?'

'Don't be cruel.' She pushed back against his too-powerful persuasiveness. 'It's over, Alessandro. It has to be. I'm sorry if its inconvenient, or embarrassing for your reputation…but I can't go on like this.'

'Like what? What is so awful about this? You hate going out with me? You hate the way I make you orgasm?' he growled. 'We're living as a married couple. We're out every night, displaying our relationship.'

She recoiled in complete mortification. Was *that* why he'd taken her out? Was it all part of the act? Those moments when he'd looked at her he'd intended his friends to see it? Had that been part of his performance?

Too late she remembered he'd told her right at the start that she'd have to fake it.

'I don't want to live a lie any more. You never wanted to be my husband. You don't love me. But I've fallen for you, Alessandro,' she muttered sadly.

He stared at her, frozen for a moment, then dropped his hands to his sides. 'You're confused, *dolcezza*. This is just a crush…'

'A crush? What do you think I am? Eternally naive

because I never had a boyfriend before you?' She felt sick. 'And what am I to you? Just another notch on your bedpost?'

'Katie—'

'Don't *minimise* what's between us. Tell the truth.'

'We're...having an affair.'

'Right.' She curled her hands so tightly together her nails almost pierced her palms. 'You *never* wanted to marry me—not even pretend. And you shouldn't have. You just felt sorry for me that night when I panicked...' She dragged in another burning breath. 'You want to be free and you can be. I can too.'

'I did what you asked of me. I did *everything.*'

'And I never should have asked you. I didn't know what you'd been through.'

'What's that supposed to mean?' His expression shut down.

'You don't want to love because you don't want to be hurt. And I get it. You lost everyone. Your mother died. You saw your father's heart break in front of your eyes. Then you lost your home and him and everything he'd worked for. Love has brought nothing but loss to you.'

'*This* is not love.'

'Not for you, no. But don't deny my feelings. Don't deny what I'm saying.'

'I *do* deny it. You're just bewitched by my looks— what was it you said? I don't even need to open my mouth?'

His cruel rejection of her affection hurt. Because it was a denial not just of her but of his own real worth. Or did he think she was too stupid to see what was really in front of her?

'It's not that, Alessandro. Nor is it your money or

your power. It is *you*. Your discipline, your insane work ethic, but also your compassion, your belief in me. You *have* done everything I've asked—because you're loyal and protective. Yes, it's also your sensuality…you know it is…but most of all it's just *you*. You're impossible, but you always make me laugh, you always lift me up…' She gazed at him and the truth whispered out. 'You've made my life so much more than fun. I love how I feel when I'm around you.'

He didn't move. 'If I'm all that, why won't you stay?'

'Because you deserve better too,' she said huskily. 'You deserve not just to be loved, but to feel this kind of love for someone else.' She blinked away the burn of tears. 'You don't invest in anything. Not really. Not relationships, not even companies. You enjoy the game— the chase, the catch… And when you're done you flick them on. You're never emotionally invested in anything except the memories on your island.'

In his pale face his eyes flashed wildly. 'Have you finished critiquing me?'

Her anger sparked. 'Sorry, are you bored already? That's your usual get-out excuse, right?'

'Katie—'

'This is the last thing you want, isn't it? This terrifies you—someone who truly loves you. But don't worry. I won't die of a broken heart. Don't feel guilty about hurting me.'

He flinched.

'But really *you're* the one who doesn't want to get hurt. Fair enough.'

'No, Katie. You're reading into things that aren't there.' He shook his head dismissively. 'You're just

tired. It's been a whirlwind… It won't be this intense
for ever. It never is.'

His denial shocked her. It was as if he hadn't heard
a word she'd said. Because he didn't feel the way she
did. 'So let me leave now, then.'

His jaw tensed. She watched ice harden his eyes.

'You can't give me a real reason to stay,' she said
softly.

It seemed he couldn't say anything. He'd frozen.

She waited as a last little spark of hope flickered before fading. 'You never wanted to marry anyone. No
marriage. No kids. No love. No drama.'

He still didn't reply—didn't say the words she desperately wanted to hear. Of course he didn't. She wasn't
enough. He wouldn't want her for ever. No one ever had.
Not even Susan needed her now…

Katie had never felt so alone.

And now he literally stepped back from her.

'What are you going to do?' he asked.

'I need to get out and live—see and do everything
I've missed out on for so long.'

'What can you do without me?' He glared at her. '*No
one* can give you what I can give you.'

'But you can't give me what I really want. You know
you can't.'

He flung his head up, as if he scented danger. 'So
you want to meet someone else?'

'Eventually, yes.' She wanted to find someone who'd
fall in love with *her*. Just for her.

He looked furious. 'Not while we're still married—'

'Don't worry, it's going to take me a while to get
over you.'

She blinked back tears, because the thought of finding someone else appalled her. But he wasn't going to stop her. Because he wasn't going to say what wasn't true.

'I don't want to accept less than I deserve. And I don't want to use you any more.'

His jaw clenched. 'I'm *helping* you.'

'No, I'm *using* you, Alessandro.'

He hated the thought that she had any control over him in this. She drew in another breath.

'I'm not going to be like my family. But I'm not going to be like you either. You're kind, but you're also a coward. Life hurts. Love hurts. We lose people along the way, we get rejected, and it hurts. But not you—not any more, right? Because you avoid possibilities, chances. Your entire existence is as fake as our marriage. You have so much more to offer someone, but you choose not to. It's such a waste.'

'We had a deal—'

'Just be *honest*!' she cried. 'You don't love me. You don't want to be married. You never did. You need to let me go.'

CHAPTER FOURTEEN

IT TOOK ALESSANDRO a moment to realise that the loud ringing noise in the room was coming from his pocket, not inside his head. He'd ignored it for so long it had gone to voicemail, but less than three seconds later it began ringing again. With far less co-ordination than usual he pulled out his phone and glanced at the screen. He'd never been so glad to get an urgent call.

'Really?' Katie gaped, fury lighting her eyes. 'You're going to answer that *now*?'

'It might be important,' he muttered.

'And this conversation isn't?'

It wasn't a 'conversation' they'd been having. 'I just need a minute.'

Alessandro stalked into his study, slamming the door behind him and answering the phone as he went. He barely heard Dominique's query about a major deal that suddenly seemed utterly unimportant. He couldn't even answer. He couldn't tolerate the torrent of emotions Katie's stormy outrage had unleashed. He couldn't think.

'I'll call you back later.'

He abruptly ended the call to Dominque and took a breath. It didn't help. Why was Katie so determined to destroy what was a perfectly good thing? Why stir up stuff that didn't need to be—?

He turned and strode back to the lounge, pausing on the threshold. It was empty. One icy thought sliced through the chaos. He immediately glanced down the hall. Yes, her hold-all bag had gone. He quickly checked the other rooms in the apartment, even though he knew. Half her clothes still hung in the walk-in wardrobe she'd used. The ice inside him began to burn.

He crossed to the window overlooking the street— two taxis were waiting at the rank over the road. She'd have had no trouble getting a ride. Or she might have headed for the train station around the corner... It didn't really matter. All that mattered was that she'd gone.

He discovered the note in the kitchen. A single sheet of paper on the counter, a single line written on it.

Thanks for everything.

Her words coldly echoed the warning he'd given her that night he'd taken her to his bed for the first time... *'I can't give you everything.'*

He scowled. When had she written this? He'd been out of the room so briefly. She must have snatched her bag and sprinted. She couldn't have stopped to scrawl a message. Had she written this before, because she'd actually intended to leave without saying goodbye? He'd returned home earlier than he'd meanat to because he'd been unable to stay away...

And she'd been unable to give him even one more minute.

Rage erupted. How dared she? When he'd done everything she'd asked of him? More, in fact.

He phoned her—naturally she didn't answer. He didn't leave a message. He paced the floor. Then phoned again. And again.

Sheer fury and shock made it impossible to process anything properly.

Apparently she'd made a stand and moved to get on with her own life. She'd fought for the independence and freedom she'd never had. Good for her, right? But *he* wasn't her enemy.

'I can't stay here with you.'

That was so unjust. He wasn't cruel. She'd said he needed to let her go. She'd said it would hurt her to stay. He couldn't believe that—they were getting on well. Really well. It was all just fine…wasn't it?

But then she'd said she loved him.

His innards iced all over again. She did *not*. Every cell rejected that. It was gratitude. Because she'd had so little kindness in her life she was mistaking her response to his actions. He'd helped her and she was overly appreciative because she wasn't used to it.

And it *was* a kind of crush. Her want for him was hormone-driven—she'd discovered she liked sex. It wasn't *love*. She was too inexperienced to know any different. She was naive and sheltered and she was confused.

How had he gone from not wanting to mess with her to messing everything up? *He* wasn't naive or sheltered and yet he was completely confused.

Liar.

He slumped into a chair and stared moodily out of the window.

He knew exactly what had happened. Everything

he'd happily avoided all his adult life. Emotional intensity. Vulnerability. Real *risk*.

Maybe she was right to say he'd never invested that most valuable part of himself. Not his heart. And why was that? Because he'd never wanted to care so particularly for one person that if they left he'd be wrecked.

He'd been wrecked before when he'd lost his parents and his home. He'd rebuilt himself. Now he had power and privilege and the capacity to do pretty much what he wanted. He had everything, didn't he? And he'd been perfectly happy until she'd come along. And then he'd been happy with how things had been between them... they'd been *good*.

Why had she ruined it? Why had she pushed? What was so wrong with how things had been?

Unable to rest, he worked round the clock. Unable to socialise, he ignored calls from Vassily and the others. He would've gone to Italy and immersed himself in the island—except it was now permeated with her presence and he couldn't bear the thought of feeling this emptiness there.

He prowled around his apartment like a wounded beast. She was constantly in his thoughts, in his dreams, in his aching heart...

It would get better. Things always did.

But two days later it wasn't improving any.

Not almost a week later either.

Slowly he realised that for all the challenge in his work, for all the wealth he'd accumulated, he had nothing he really wanted to *hold*. The one thing he wanted had walked out on him.

His 'amazing lifestyle' had merely been masking an empty core. Katie had ripped off the façade and exposed that painful truth to the light. He'd refused to give himself fully. Not for him that all-consuming, life-changing, bigger-than-both-of-them love… He'd never wanted that. So he'd never let anyone in. Deliberately cut relationships off at the knees.

But then Katie had catapulted into his life and he hadn't been able to cut her off. He'd been unable to say no to her on almost anything. She'd exposed him, and she'd also soothed him. She'd made him feel so much that was good. But he'd been wary and defensive, and so focused on staying his precious bulletproof self he'd not given her what she really needed. Even when she'd finally braved up enough to ask for it.

'You don't want to be hurt.'

He'd scoffed at her words at the time. But she was right.

'Coward.'

When she'd thrown that at him he'd frozen, his action proving her accusation in that exact moment. She'd not asked for much—only to know his feelings—but he'd remained silent, denying her. He realised now what a betrayal that silence had been. The same betrayal she'd had for years. Her foster-father had never told her she was loved, safe, wanted…

He'd done the worst thing possible to her. And hurting her had been horrific.

He was an idiot, and now he was suffering the kind of pain he realised he'd spent half his life trying to avoid. And he was such a fool because he hadn't even let himself have the flipside of that risk. He hadn't had all the good things—*time* with her. Love. Laughter… All that contentment and possibility.

She wanted *family*. And she should have it. She

should have a husband who adored her, who could fill her life with children and all the warmth and laughter she'd missed out on.

He'd thought he'd never want any of that. He'd thought he'd remain free for ever. But it turned out he wasn't 'free'—he was lost. He'd been enjoying affair after affair, as superficial as she'd once suggested. And that judgement of hers had only hit so hard because it was true.

For once he let himself sift through those memories he would never normally recall—the happiness and joy of his parents. Watching them, being loved by them, bathed in security. He'd been so fortunate to have had it at all. Katie hadn't had any of that. Yet she was the most loving, generous, loyal person he'd met. And so courageous.

Only now she'd run away. And she only ran when she felt she had no other choice. When she was too hurt, too scared to fight.

He had to fight for her.

He had to ensure she had everything she wanted and needed.

He had to be the one to give it to her.

Because he wanted—needed—it from her as well.

Actually, he just wanted her. He'd never wanted anything or anyone more. But when she'd told him she loved him he'd frozen. Not only denying himself, but denying *her*. His pain worsened. Not for his past, but for his future—his *now*. He'd *failed* her.

But that didn't mean he was going to *quit*.

Energy and determination surged through his body.

He'd find her. He'd fight for her. And he'd damn well bring her back and tell her *his* truth—that she was his heart.

CHAPTER FIFTEEN

KATIE THREADED THROUGH the crowd of tourists as she headed towards her hostel. The café where she'd been working for the last few days was busy and she was tired. Hopefully that meant she might actually sleep tonight. Because while the long working days were good, they didn't stop her from thinking about Alessandro all the time, and the small hours alone and awake at night were the worst.

'I've finally found you.'

'Oh!' She lurched to a stop in the middle of the footpath.

'Sorry. I didn't mean to give you a fright.'

Alessandro had materialised out of nowhere. Tall, stubbled, intense and far too intimidating, in black trousers and an open-collared shirt.

Slack-jawed, she stared. A too-powerful thud walloped her heart. 'What are you doing here?'

'How could you just vanish?'

She blinked rapidly at the reproach in his eyes. 'I didn't mean to worry you.'

'Didn't you?' Anger flashed across his face. 'Or did you think so little of me you thought I wouldn't worry at all?'

She swallowed as her anger surged in response. She'd told him what she thought of him and he'd dismissed it as a *crush*.

'Why run away and hide?' he growled. 'You said all those things and didn't give me the chance to—' He broke off and visibly sought for control. 'I thought I could keep this… I don't think I can.' He jerked his head in the direction of the hostel. 'You're staying there?'

She nodded.

'Living the life you've missed out on until now?' His lips compressed.

'Living a life, yes. Working at a job I got for myself, spending money I've earned.'

He gazed at her for a moment, and slowly the faintest suggestion of a smile flickered in his eyes. Then he took a careful breath. 'I'm in the hotel across the road. Will you come there so we can talk?'

'You have something to say now?' she asked smartly.

'As it happens, I do. I'll do it here if I have to, but I think we'd both prefer some privacy.'

Heat flared, skimming over not just her skin but every muscle, every organ. That electricity had always been a strong current within her and she had to resist. 'I don't think that's wise.'

'I thought you'd discovered your courage, Katie?' he dared softly.

She stared back at him, knowing how much he enjoyed challenging her. How much she enjoyed it too. His expression slowly altered, revealing something more—something she truly didn't have the courage to face.

'Give me a chance, *dolcezza*.'

And that she couldn't resist. Even though she was

more terrified than at any time in her life. Not even Brian's worst threats had made her feel this vulnerable.

Hardly aware, she crossed the street with him. The silence simmered, thickening the air while time twisted. Her pulse raced but her breathing felt slow, and all of a sudden they were alone.

His hotel suite was too quiet, too small for comfort despite its opulent spaciousness. She crossed the room to the window and looked down at the bustling Edinburgh streets as her panic rose.

What was the point in this? Why rehash that pain of what had been said...and not said?

She wasn't ready to face him. Why did seeing him now hurt even more than when she'd walked out?

'Katie?'

She closed her eyes against the soft contrition she heard in his voice. This wasn't what she wanted.

'Katie, I'm sorry—'

'Don't *pity* me,' Katie whispered sharply, screwing her eyes closed. It was too much.

'Actually, I've been feeling sorry for myself.'

He'd moved closer—she could feel him right behind her. But she didn't turn and face him. She didn't want to listen.

'I've had a chance to think...' he added slowly. 'And I think I like being married.'

Her heart lurched, and then anger scorched it. 'Go find someone you *want* to marry, then,' she wheezed.

'I already have.' He put his hands on her shoulders. 'Katie, *dolcezza*, breathe.'

She couldn't step back—couldn't escape. 'Don't...'

She shook her head, glancing over her shoulder—beyond him—to the door so far across the room.

'Don't run away again.' He applied a little pressure until she pivoted to face him. 'I let you down with my silence the other day and I'm sorry for that. I just... I was just so stunned. Please don't run away. Stay so we can talk.' He drew in a shaking breath. 'I needed time before you left. I need just a little more now.'

Her flare of defiance faded. Her whole body hurt too much—her throat felt so tight she couldn't speak. He looked more serious than she'd ever seen him, the blue of his eyes deep and almost bruised.

'You've been waiting all your life for someone to love you the way you ought to be loved. I am so sorry I've made you wait longer.'

Her eyes suddenly filled. Stinging unwanted tears that she had to hide, even as she ached to lean forward and wrap her arms around him, to forgive him anything, accept anything, and never let him go no matter what. She wanted to *hope*.

But she couldn't let herself. She couldn't even look at him.

'Please, don't...' Swallowing hard, she wrapped her arms around her waist and bent her head to stare hard at the floor.

He cupped her face in hands so gentle it was as if he were afraid she might disappear before his eyes. It was the lightest of caresses that compelled her to look back up at him.

'*Dolcezza*, don't cry.'

'You shouldn't have come here. You shouldn't have...' She looked into his blue eyes and a tear slipped down her cheek. 'It's not fair.'

'Life isn't always fair, is it? Sometimes we win, sometimes we lose. Sometimes we just run away.' He edged nearer, his voice dropping. 'And sometimes we throw the game because we're afraid of winning.' He shook his head ever so slightly. 'I threw the game, Katie. And I wasn't fair to either of us. I couldn't be honest with you before because I couldn't be honest with myself. I couldn't bear to face how much you mattered to me.'

She couldn't keep up—couldn't accept what she thought he was trying to say. She only heard the resistance. 'You don't want to care about me.' And it hurt *so* much.

'I didn't want to care about anyone.'

He didn't deny it, but he didn't let her go. Rather he stepped nearer, until his eyes were only inches from hers and his breath warmed her face.

'I didn't even realise how safe I was playing. I thought I had it all figured out. But you were right. I was just afraid. Underneath it all I was empty—maybe I'd never got past that hurt from years ago. But I thought I could handle you. I thought I was doing you a favour—what a hero, right? The truth was I wanted you and I knew you wanted me. I thought it could be an affair like any other…'

'It *was* an affair.' She made herself say it. 'Our marriage was never real.'

'Actually, it was. It *is*.' He brushed away her tear with the backs of his fingers in the lightest of touches. 'Our feelings are real, Katie.' He gazed at her. 'My feelings are real.'

Her eyes filled all over again and she rapidly blinked. 'Don't—'

'You were too generous in saying I'd sought solace in the past… I think I was being selfish. I avoided getting close to anyone, subconsciously protecting my heart, because…poor me… I'd been hurt. But who hasn't in life? I was just taking what I wanted and giving little in return. I was a jerk.'

His self-recrimination shocked her. '*No*. You were just…*living*. And then you helped me. You did everything I asked of you—' It was just that she'd asked for too much.

'Only the easy things—money, sex… But real caring? The way *you* care for people?' He leaned closer. 'I didn't even realise what that was until you showed me. Not until I was doing it for you without even realising—'

'I don't want you to feel you have to take care of me any more,' she interrupted fiercely. 'I don't want you to rescue me.'

'Who's rescuing who, Katie?' he asked.

A gorgeous rueful smile flitted across his face before he became more serious than ever.

'The day you left you asked me to be honest, and at the time I couldn't be.' He huffed out a harsh breath. 'Now I *have* to be. You were right. I've been a coward. I hurt you in the worst possible way. I hurt you by my silence. Because you have the capacity for the kind of love that terrifies me. The kind that is so huge, so deep, that you'd do almost anything for someone you love. The kind of love my parents had. The kind I've secretly always craved but never wanted to admit. The kind I have for you.'

A rushing noise in her ears muffled his words. She couldn't tell if what she was hearing was… What had he said? The soaring sensation inside threatened to make her faint.

'I love you, Katie. The best kind of all,' he muttered. 'It isn't a game, *dolcezza*. It's real. And it's everything.'

She swayed and he caught her around the waist, pulling her flush against him.

The sigh she released was jagged and painful. 'What did you say?'

'I know it's going to take a while for you to believe me. That's okay. I'm not going anywhere. Because I can't be without you. I can't believe I let you go. These days have been hell.' Emotion shook not just his voice but his body, and he pressed her closer still. 'You're not walking out on me ever again and I'm never walking out on you.'

His kiss burned through the dizziness. He was here and he wanted her and what he'd said was real.

Katie gasped as his passion swept through her and she soared. There was so much emotion in his touch, in his broken apologies. He was so powerful, so possessive as he pulled her closer, his hands raking down her body as if he couldn't quite believe she was there, melting into him.

But suddenly he pulled back.

'What…?' She couldn't quite breathe enough to get the words out.

He too seemed breathless, his chest rising and falling fast as he reached into his pocket.

'On the way up here I thought maybe we could have another wedding ceremony…one we put a little more thought into. We could invite Susan and our friends. I'd like to wear a decent suit. You could wear the dress of your dreams…'

Katie couldn't move.

'I need you to understand that I *choose* you, Katie. I

love you and I want you alongside me always. So will you marry me all over again?' He opened the box. 'Will you mean it with me this time?'

He wanted to marry her again? He wanted to show his feelings for her to their world?

'You don't need to...' Katie saw the ring and winced. 'You've given me too much already.'

She didn't want any more of his money. She didn't want him to think he had to do these big things for her. She wanted only him.

'Not everything Katie. Not yet. You've given me more.' He took the ring from the box. 'You're everything to me. And I want to celebrate it. I want the world to know.'

'Alessandro...' Her heart burst—he wanted to publicly profess his feelings for her, claim her as his? A rush of warmth and pride and pleasure overwhelmed her.

'It's...'

He slid the ring down her finger. 'A perfect fit.'

The diamond sparkled so brightly she had to blink again. Rapidly. 'You didn't have to—'

'I wanted to. Accept the gift, Katie.'

He kept hold of her hand and smiled at her. It wasn't the wicked, amused smile of always—it had something else in it as well. Something infinitely more.

'If you need to find confidence in me you can look at this and remember. And I like seeing you adorned in my gifts. It gives me a sense of security. I figure it wards off other men.'

She couldn't help a little chuckle, and then she shook her head to try to stop those tears from falling again. 'What other men?'

'You have no idea how beautiful you are,' he teased

gently, then tugged at her hand to pull her back into his arms. He caressed the length of her spine to pull her closer still. 'So let me tell you.'

Her eyes filled, but he tilted her chin so she couldn't hide her face again.

'Listen, *dolcezza*—listen and believe. You need to know you're more than gorgeous. Your hair shines, and so does your skin, and your eyes are truly bewitching... all those colours in them gleam. But you light up with this kind of magic.' He angled his head. 'There's no one else with your vitality, your generosity—'

'Alessandro—'

'It's true. And I know you won't believe me yet, because you've never been told before, you've never really been shown. But I'll tell you, and I'll show you, every day for the rest of our lives. I love you, Katie, and I will never leave you.'

He knew just what she needed to hear. Because he knew her. He understood her. And he'd come for her. It meant everything.

She hugged him back tightly and instantly he cradled her closer.

'I thought relationships weren't worth it.' He closed his eyes. 'But *you're* worth it. Being with you, having you, then losing you...' He groaned. 'Never leave me again, Katie. It was the absolute worst.' He gazed deeply into her eyes. 'Stay with me always. Love me always.'

His vulnerability broke her open. Because he'd been hurt in the past, he'd been lonely and so had she.

'I'm yours,' she admitted on a shaky sigh. 'I'll always be yours.'

'I've missed you so much, *dolcezza*,' he whispered.

He gave her what she needed—his touch, his kiss. She breathed him in and began truly to believe.

He didn't hurry, instead undertaking the most tender rediscovery of her body. He murmured constantly—how much he'd missed her, how much he loved her—in English, in Italian, in his touch. And when he finally claimed his place in her body and soul she sobbed in sheer ecstasy.

It wasn't a mere escape or a moment of pleasure. It was so much more. Their intimacy deepened as the last knot locking her heart away loosened. Joy surged within, like lightning that transcended the physical. He had all of her—but he held her with such care, such reverence. It was tenderness and passion and a promise of pure security.

She finally understood how much he cared. And it was a long, long time before either of them could speak again.

It was Alessandro who lifted his head from where he'd been resting on her breast and sent her a teasing smile. 'You smell delicious.'

She giggled. 'I spent the afternoon baking cinnamon buns.'

Laughing, he lowered his head and nuzzled her neck, as if he couldn't get enough of her taste. 'Come home and make something for yourself.'

'I'd like that. I think I'd like to start afresh. Not White Oaks, not Zetticci. Something completely new.' She quivered a little inside at the excitement of the prospect. 'Will you help me?'

'Try and stop me.' He nipped her skin with his teeth and tugged her closer to him again, pressing against her intimately. 'We could build lots of things together. A company, a home, a family…'

'You really want all that with me?'

'More than I've ever wanted anything,' he said simply.

She melted, welcoming him completely.

They were more than a match—they were a *team*.

'*Ti amo*,' she whispered shyly.

He stilled and she saw pure vulnerability flash in his eyes as he blinked rapidly. '*Dolcezza—*'

'Accept the gift, Alessandro,' she challenged softly.

He nodded. 'If I have you I have everything,' he said. 'You *are* everything.'

She finally believed that she meant that much to him. He treasured her just as she treasured him.

He slowly traced a gentle path over her heart with the tips of his fingers. She'd never felt as close to anyone, never as safe, never as content.

She smiled past her own tears and kissed him again. Together they'd soften old scars. Together they'd create new joy.

And together they would always, *always*, love.

* * * * *

If you enjoyed
The Innocent's Emergency Wedding
by Natalie Anderson
you're sure to enjoy these other
Conveniently Wed! stories!

Untamed Billionaire's Innocent Bride
by Caitlin Crews
Bought Bride for the Argentinian
by Sharon Kendrick
Contracted as His Cinderella Bride
by Heidi Rice
Shock Marriage for the Powerful Spaniard
by Cathy Williams

Available now

#3765 UNWRAPPING THE INNOCENT'S SECRET
Secret Heirs of Billionaires
by Caitlin Crews
It infuriates self-made billionaire Pascal that he can't forget the forbidden passion he once shared with innocent Cecilia. This Christmas, he's determined to shake off those memories... until they shockingly come face-to-face—and Cecilia reveals her six-year secret!

#3766 CLAIMING MY HIDDEN SON
The Notorious Greek Billionaires
by Maya Blake
My marriage to Calypso was simply business—until our unexpectedly passionate wedding night! Unwilling to muddy our convenient arrangement, I left. Now discovering the baby in my estranged wife's arms, I will claim my son—and Calypso, too...

#3767 BRIDE BEHIND THE BILLION-DOLLAR VEIL
Crazy Rich Greek Weddings
by Clare Connelly
To complete his empire, fantastically wealthy Thanos must counter his scandalous reputation—with a wife! His assistant, Alice, is the perfect choice. Until he lifts her veil and their intense, electrifying kiss complicates *everything*...

#3768 THE ITALIAN'S CHRISTMAS PROPOSITION
by Cathy Williams
When Matteo's rescue of Rosie puts his business deal in jeopardy, he sees only one solution—making her his fake fiancée! But will their unexpected connection tempt Matteo to put a ring on Rosie's finger—for real?

Get 4 FREE REWARDS!

We'll send you 2 FREE Books plus 2 FREE Mystery Gifts.

"Señor Navarro," she said, offering her hand.

"Angelo," he corrected. His clasp sent electricity through to her nerve endings as he took the liberty of greeting her with "Pia."

"Thank you for coming," she said, desperately pretending they were strangers when all she could think about was how his weight had pressed her into the cushions while her entire being had seemed to fly.

His eyes dazzled yet pinned her in place. There was an air of aggression about him. Hostility even, in the way he had appeared like this, when she had literally been on the defensive. He seemed ready for a fight.

She had almost hoped he would leave her hanging after her note. She could have raised their baby with a clear conscience that she had tried to reach out, while facing no interference from this unknown quantity.

As for what would happen if he did get in touch? She had tried to be realistic in her expectations, but Poppy had stuck a few delusions in her head. They seemed even more ridiculous as she faced such a daunting conversation with him. How had she even found the courage to say such frank things that night, let alone do the things they'd done? Wicked, intimate, carnal things that caused a blush to singe up from her throat into her cheeks.

"I need a moment," she said, voice straining.

She had already declined invitations for drinks, fearful her avoidance of a glass of champagne would make her condition obvious. She only had to say a last goodbye to the committee and

"Thank you again, but I must take this meeting."

Moments later, trembling inwardly, she led Angelo into the small office off the lab where she had worked the past three years when not in the field. She had already packed her things into a small cardboard box, which sat on the chair. She was shifting from academic work to motherhood and marriage. That was all that was left of her former life.

Angelo seemed to eat up all the air as he closed the door behind him and looked at the empty bulletin board, the box of tissues and the well-used filing cabinet.

Pia started to move the box, but he said, "I'll stand."

He was taller than her, which made him well over six feet, because she had the family's genetic disposition toward above-average height. His air of watchfulness was intimidating, too, especially when he trained his laser-blue eyes on her again.

"Your card was very cryptic," he said.

She had spent a long time composing it, wondering why he had sneaked into the ball when he could easily have afforded the plate fee. At the time, she had thought his reason for being on the rooftop was exactly as he had explained it—curiosity. She had many more questions now, but didn't ask them yet. There was every chance she would never see him again after she told him why she had reached out.

Memories of their intimacy that night accosted her daily. It was top of mind now, which put her at a further disadvantage. Her only recourse was to do what she always did when she was uncomfortable—hide behind a curtain of reserve and speak her piece as matter-of-factly as possible.

"I'll come straight to the point." She hitched her hip on the edge of her desk and set her clammy palms together, affecting indifference while fighting to keep a quaver from her voice.

"I'm pregnant. It's yours."

Don't miss
Bound by Their Nine-Month Scandal
available November 2019 wherever
Harlequin Presents® books and eBooks are sold.

www.Harlequin.com

HARLEQUIN

Presents®

Coming next month—*USA TODAY* bestselling author
Sharon Kendrick's festive marriage of convenience! In
His Contract Christmas Bride, billionaire Drakon *must*
marry. Yet his convenient bride is about to spark a
not-so-convenient desire...

As the new guardian to his orphaned nephew, wealthy CEO
Drakon must marry! And sweet, caring Lucy is the ideal
candidate. But all emotionally scarred Drakon can offer is a
lavish Christmas wedding—and nights of tantalizing pleasure!
While Lucy accepts and loves being a stand-in mother, she
soon realizes she can't be just a wife in name only. Can guarded
Drakon give anything more to his contract bride?

His Contract Christmas Bride

Conveniently Wed!

Available November 2019

HPBPA1019

5665